I0660627

Myron Coloney

Manomin : a rhythmical romance of Minnesota, the great rebellion, and the Minnesota massacres, by Myron Coloney

Myron Coloney

Manomin : a rhythmical romance of Minnesota, the great rebellion, and the Minnesota massacres, by Myron Coloney

ISBN/EAN: 9783743328648

Manufactured in Europe, USA, Canada, Australia, Japa

Cover: Foto ©Andreas Hilbeck / pixelio.de

Manufactured and distributed by brebook publishing software (www.brebook.com)

Myron Coloney

Manomin : a rhythmical romance of Minnesota, the great rebellion, and the Minnesota massacres, by Myron Coloney

MANOMIN:

A

RHYTHMICAL ROMANCE OF MINNESOTA,

THE GREAT REBELLION

AND THE

MINNESOTA MASSACRES.

BY MYRON COLONEY.

ST. LOUIS:
PUBLISHED BY THE AUTHOR.
1866.

Entered according to Act of Congress. in the year 1865, by

.MYRON COLONEY,.

In the Clerk's Office of the United States District Court,

For the Eastern District of Missouri.

A. WIEBUSCH & SON,

Stereotypers & Printers,

St. Louis, Mo.

IN MEMORIAM.

DIED — In the month of September 1864, at UNION FARM, near Rolla, Phelps County, Mo., stricken down by the bullet of a Missouri bushwhacker, while with his rifle, "Biting Betty," in hand he was bravely defending the home and family of the author of this book from pillage and assault, brave and noble Uncle ANDREAS M. DARLING, in the fifty-eighth year of his age.

———◦◦◦———

IN the year 1858, myself and wife emigrated from the city of Chicago, Ill., to Douglas County, Minn., and settled upon the lovely shores of Lake Ida. Douglas County is about one hundred and sixty miles north-west from St. Paul, and is reached by travelling up the valley of the Mississippi River to St. Cloud, the head of navigation, thence up the Sauk River Valley in an almost westerly direction to Osakis Lake, where the eastern boundary of the county begins. Alexandria, the county-seat and post-office town of the county, is about twelve miles further on from Osakis Lake, and Lake Ida is distant from Alexandria about six miles, still further on toward Breckinridge and Abercrombie, on the great Red River of the North.

At the time myself and wife moved into Douglas County there was no beaten road over the prairie further than the little paper town of Kandotta, near Fairy Lake. One log cabin, and a very indifferent one at that, had been erected upon this site, a liberty pole put up, a pole stable built and the "town" had an existence and a name. We purchased ox-teams in St. Cloud, loaded our household goods and provisions into the wagons and the journey was commenced. It was in May and there were no bridges across the streams. The Sauk River had to be crossed four times in the journey and as it was very high, we were obliged to unload each time and after ferrying our goods over in a small skiff, take the wagon to pieces and ferry it over in the same manner.

On our journey, at every cabin we stopped at, we heard of a Mr. DARLING and his family with their teams and goods just ahead of us, bound for the same part of the State, and we hurried on expecting every night to overtake them, but the energy and experience of the hardy frontiersman widened the distance between us every day, and when we arrived at Alexandria we found he had been there some three or four days, and had immediately proceeded to his "claim" upon Lake Darling, about one mile beyond the town in the direction of Lake Ida.

Notwithstanding the lateness of the season Mr. DARLING broke up and fenced about twelve acres of land and raised a large crop of "sod corn," potatoes, buckwheat and ruta bagas. He also built himself a good, warm house, and a stable for his stock, and in farm enterprise took and kept the lead in all that section. He was a most indefatigable hunter and trapper at the season of the year when such business could be made to pay, and with old "Biting Betty" could shoot a loon's eye out forty rods distant every fire. "Biting Betty" was made to order for him in Wisconsin; she carried a half ounce ball and weighed sixteen pounds, which every sportsman ought to know is an immense weight for a rifle.

Mr. ANDREAS M. DARLING was born of poor parents on a rugged farm in the northern part of the State of New York, and his father, like himself, appears to have been a kind of a "rolling stone," always keeping ahead of "civilization." In an early day they moved to western New York, and thence to Ohio, and there young ANDREAS took the contract of cutting down the forest on the present site of Cleveland, Ohio. When settlers began to be too numerous, he moved into Michigan, where he married, thence into Wisconsin, and from there into Minnesota.

He was a large, well proportioned man, standing six feet four inches in his stockings, powerful, kind hearted and true. No man was readier at a "raising," "chopping," "logging," or "plowing," than he. He was invariably chosen as "boss" of the occasion, no matter what it might be. He was always on hand at the frequent "dances" with which the settlers, for miles around, sought to make merry the long winters of that distant, hyperborean region, and his "team" always contained the jolliest load of young folks in the settlement.

When the Sioux massacres commenced I was fortunately away from home. My wife had gone to Chicago to visit her parents, and I was travelling through Indiana purchasing sheep. My house and its contents were burned and several of the neighbors, living higher up the road, were killed.

The settlers about Alexandria organized themselves into a company, and electing Mr. DARLING captain, hastily left their homes for St. Cloud, one hundred miles below. The Indians followed and surrounded them nearly every night, but did not dare to attack, and finally the whole party reached St. Cloud in safety.

The crops had all been left standing in the fields, and the cattle, hogs and sheep were roaming at large. Assurance was given to Mr. DARLING by Governor RAMSEY that a company of soldiers should be stationed permanently at Alexandria very soon, and therefore as soon as he could find safe quarters for his family, he with a neighbor of his, Mr. BARNES, went fearlessly back to their homes and commenced saving their crops, and as soon as the soldiers came up they moved their families back again.

I never returned, but moving to St. Louis, commenced trading through south-west Missouri and Arkansas, and finally in connection with another gentleman of St. Louis, purchased the HAMILTON LENNOX plantation of a thousand acres, near Rolla, and christened it "Union Farm." It was so near Rolla, which was strongly garrisoned, that I never entertained the slightest apprehension of trouble from bushwhackers, and with my wife and father-in-law and family did not hesitate to move upon the place at once.

I had kept up a pretty regular correspondence with Mr. DARLING, and believing him to be in a good deal of danger on his claim, a mile from the stockade, I advised him to come down to Missouri and take charge of my property as overseer. As there was a drouth prevailing in Minnesota at the time and his family felt lonesome and discouraged, he consented and selling out his teams, utensils &c., came on.

I had leased the property to my father-in-law, Mr. CHAUNCEY TUTTLE, for a term of years, and he, ratifying my arrangement with Mr. DARLING, gave him full charge of the farm. All went along peaceably and well, until the month of September 1864. Myself and Mr. TUTTLE had come up to St. Louis on business and while here received the following telegram which fell upon us like a flash of lightning:

To MYRON COLONEY:

We were bushwhacked last night and Mr. DARLING was killed.

MRS. J. A. COLONEY.

Alas, it was too true! The dear, kind-hearted, brave old man was shot down while gallantly defending the entrance of my parlor. The murderers were "DICK KITCHEN'S" band of guerillas, to whom, it is alleged, the "WRIGHT boys," lately shot by Col. BABCOOKE'S men, belonged. The immediate instigators of the murder were two sons of the former owner of the place, TOM. and BILL LENNOX. They have yet to answer to the law for this most foul and hellish deed.

The military authorities at Rolla sent over an escort and brought the body of the brave old man to town, and buried him with becoming obsequies in the military burying ground. His stricken widow and her children determined to return to the "claim" in Minnesota which they did, and are there at this present time.

It is for her benefit — to assist her in meeting the severe struggle of life, deprived as she is of the manly hand and strong arm on which she was wont to rely, to assist her in the proper education of her children, that this book has been printed. I do not know that it will ever return what it cost, but I trust it will and hope it will supply a fund for many years to come to fill the purse that the energy and industry of him who was so cruelly snatched away from her was wont to fill.

She now lives upon the shores of Lake Darling in Minnesota, while the remains of her noble husband lie away down here in the soil of Missouri. It is my earnest wish to disinter the body, provide it with a suitable coffin and send it up to her, but embarrassments which have come upon me from being obliged to give up the farm, and losses in business have put it entirely out of my power to do so, at present, and if, therefore, after reading the story of the gallant, kindhearted, true old man, any one should feel disposed to enclose me a contribution for that purpose, however small, it will be duly acknowledged and appreciated.

"Biting Betty" was carried off by the party who committed the murder, as was every other thing of value in my house; but as the rifle was a very heavy one it is thought that it was left somewhere in the State, and if it can be recovered and sent to me, a large reward will be paid for it.

St. Louis, Missouri, October 1865.

MYRON COLONEY.

DEDICATION.

At my desk I sit alone,
Bathed in floods of silver-tone —
Evening vesper's soothing chime —
Musing on this work of mine.
Down life's path I turn my gaze
Backward to my boyhood days;
Then returning, closely look
Through each grotto, grove and nook,
Bower of ease and brambled wood,
Long dark walks of solitude,
Sunny banks and emerald lanes,
Sterile paths and fruitful plains,
Down each yawning, black abyss,
O'er each frightful precipice,
Everywhere my feet have trod
Since the hour I came from God;
Fain to find a friend who ne'er
Changed with fortune's changeful year;
Faithful friend, long proved and tried,
True when other friendships died;

To this friend for whom I look,
I would dedicate my book.
Here are sunny eyes asmile,
Briefly lit — a little while —
With a blast of adverse fate
They grow dark and desolate.
There are graspings of the hand,
Air and intonation bland,
Giving place to cold neglect,
Contact proudly circumspect..
Oh, my soul, and is there then
No true friendship among men?
Sadly turns my heart aside,
To my own dear fire-side,
From the many to the few;
One sits there forever true!
True in sickness as in health,
True in poverty as wealth,
True though I should go astray,
True when others turn away,
Oh, thou sunshine of my life,
Loving, tender, patient WIFE,
God's best, dearest gift to me,
I inscribe my book to thee!

PREFACE.

THIS book has been written under the most un-
favorable circumstances, occupying the *spare* hours of
some six months, for while engaged upon it I have
fulfilled the duties of Commercial Editor of the *Evening News* of this city. It has been written without
a library or even a private room in which to withdraw myself. I have had no lexicons, encyclopedias,
rhyming dictionaries, or books of reference to assist
me. Harpers' Magazine and the newspapers have
been my only helps.

I have sought no publishers as I was almost entirely
unknown as a writer, and felt there would be no prob-
ability of my getting one. I have grown up in the
West, am thoroughly inoculated with its rude, ener-
getic life and its progressive, individualizing ideas.
Of course my writings must be a true manifestation
of myself. I glory in the spirit of American Ideas

and demand for myself and claim for *all others* that *true* and perfect *equality*, both in religion and politics, that is every human being's *right on earth.*

Faith in the upward progress of the human race in spite of creeds and bigotries, is the corner-stone of my religion, and especial faith in the *people* of the United States of America is my glory and pride.

So my book is *radical* upon all subjects, casting off all the old that seems to have worn out and served its purpose, and taking up and advocating all the new that seems good and true.

I do not expect it is a great poem, I do not expect it will find favor with the rich, highly cultured minds of the East. I have chosen my characters from the common walks of life, and my story is largely a recitation of life's common events. My hero is intended as a fair type of what *free institutions* develope; a hard working, intelligent, high minded boy, a dutiful son, a true patriot springing at once to the call of his country, a free thinker, trusting his own God-given judgment to decide *all* questions for him, a brave, upright and fearless *private soldier,* an unostentatious officer and a faithful lover.

To the best of my ability I have endeavored to embellish my narration with poetical ornament and if I have failed then fail it must be, as I do not know that I can ever produce anything better. At the same time I have avoided obscureness of expression, desiring to have every sentence and figure of speech clearly understood.

I have committed no intentional plagiarism, and if there is anything in my book very similar to what some one else has written before me, I do not know it now.

Hoping that my sincerity, at least, will not be doubted, I commit this, my first and undoubtedly my last literary venture to the great ocean of the American Mind.

MYRON COLONEY.

St. Louis, Missouri, October 1865.

PART FIRST.

THE BEAUTIFUL HOME—TROUBLE—A WIFE'S DEVOTION.

DEEP within an arc of locusts, pouring forth their
    odors sweet,
Nestled little Thornton Cottage, white and dustless,
    clean and neat.
Troops of woodbines clambered fondly o'er the low
    verandah, where
RICHARD THORNTON read his paper, in the spicy
    evening air.
Graveled walks and beds of flowers, sweet exotics,
    rich and rare,
Racks of fruits and blushing berries formed his
    beautiful parterre.
Plots of vines and clustering bushes, round the rear
    fence climbing high,
Told of luxuries, whose freshness money sometimes
    fails to buy.

Every threader of the highway paused before that
      quiet cot, —

Paused in wishful contemplation of that soul-enticing
      spot,

Gazed, until their weary spirits longed to flee the
      outward din

To the peaceful, sweet valhalla, to the paradise
      within!

RICHARD loved his little cottage, dearly loved its
      quiet rest,

Gowned and slippered and surrounded by the fledg-
      lings of his nest.

HARRY THORNTON was his eldest — fifteen summers,
      bright as gold,

On his shining scroll of being had their sunny
      names enrolled.

If a stainless soul from heaven — purer than eter-
      nal day —

Brighter than a diamond cluster, e'er was plucked
      and wrapped in clay,

Surely it was HARRY THORNTON's — looking from
      those earnest eyes, —

Truthful, loving, ever rising upward to its native
      skies.

Next was JESSIE, sunny-headed, sweet and simple
      as her name,

Lovely little bud of glory, tinged with blue and
      touched with flame!

Delicate as angel music, floating through a spirit
  bower,
Pensive as the sense of being in the souls most
  blessed hour!
Then there was another presence that embodied all
  his love,
Brimmed with pleasure all his senses like a blessing from above;
Hither, thither, — moving softly, every touch impart-
  ing grace,
Blended with an air of comfort everywhere about
  the place,
Wife and partner of his bosom — mother of his
  little brood,
Sweet disperser of his sorrows — sunshine of each
  darker mood,
Sunny-hearted, gentle Esther, always quiet, always
  neat,
Sure to have his arm-chair ready, gown, and slip-
  pers for his feet,
Sure to meet him with a welcome shining from her
  winsome face,
Sure to twine her white arms round him in a trustful, fond embrace.
Oh, a true and gentle woman — more than Iris'
  seven-hued span
Typifies God's love and mercy — is his dearest gift
  to man!

There was still another presence, bent in form,
   white-haired and thin,

'Twixt whose ripe and longing spirit, and the
   brighter life within,

But a segment of a cycle yet remained, a bar at
   best —

But a short step to that country, where the weary
   are at rest.

Esther's father, loved and honored by the household,
   one and all,

Spirit-pure, and meekly patient — waited but the
   bugle call

That should bid him on to glory — marshal him in
   grand array

With the gathering hosts of planets, bannered by
   eternal day!

Who could wonder then that Richard — toiling,
   planning all day long,

Joyed to see the twilight falling, joyed to hear the
   cricket's song?

That, then locking care behind him, he, with bounding heart and feet,

To his cottage and his dear ones might go flying
   down the street!

To the casual observer Richard's was an envied
   lot;

But each heart hath secret troubles which the
   stranger knoweth not.

For the world is full of shadows, creeping round
    the sunniest door,
And each hearth-stone hath its phantoms, grimly
    wrought upon the floor!
One sad evening RICHARD tarried — came not, still,
    the hour was late
When at length the waiting ESTHER heard his foot-
    steps at the gate.
Tenderly she flew to meet him, love all beaming
    in her face,
But he startled her with: " ESTHER, we must leave
    this dear old place!
That vile serpent in our Eden — that Appollyon in
    our path,
Has poured out upon us, darling, all the vials of
    his wrath.
He has bought those notes of HARVEY and my
    cottage deed-of-trust;
Times are close, I cannot pay them, so he grinds
    me in the dust!
How he chuckled as the sheriff closed my little
    store to-day,
Hissing: "' You may thank your ESTHER!'" as I
    turned to go away.
I was leaving more in sorrow than in anger, till
    the sound
Of this stinging insult smote me, then I felled him
    to the ground!

Oh, I know that it was shameful thus to yield to
    passion's blast,

But I must have struck him, ESTHER, had that
    moment been my last.

In the Syracuse House parlor I have held a long
    debate

With the BALDWINS and the CROUSES that is why I
    came so late.

They are friends of ours, my darling, and will help
    us to depart,

Never dreaming that their kindness is our bitterness
    of heart!

Oh, to leave our little cottage, where our lives were
    knit in one,

Where those gifts of God, our children, first beheld
    the light of sun,

Where so long we've turned together gilded leaves
    of golden years:

Is a bitterness that wrings me, but we have no time
    for tears!

We are young yet, ESTHER, darling, God will streng-
    then us to go;

And withdraw ourselves forever from the venom of
    our foe.

In the distant Minnesota, where the skies are ever
    blue,

We will seek the quiet border and begin our lives
    anew.

We will settle on the margin of some sweet pellucid
    lake,

That shall sing its liquid sonnets to the listening fern
    and brake,

And our house shall be embowered in a grove of
    maple-trees,

Where the breezes chaunt forever their æolian har-
    monies.

Neighbors soon will gather round us and we shall
    not be alone;

Then imploring God to bless us let us hasten and
    be gone.

We will pack up all our carpets, your piano, and
    my books,

And our furniture to charm us by its old familiar
    looks;

We will spend a day in making all our friends a
    final call,

And will stop and see Niagara Falls while jour-
    neying to St. Paul!

Will you go with me, my ESTHER, oh what say
    you, loving wife?

Is this too great a sacrifice for him you took for
    life?

Oh! I see, your heart is weeping, for the tears
    drop from your eye;

There! We will not think of going, darling ESTHER,
    do not cry!"

" You mistake my sorrow, RICHARD, oh, most gladly
   will I go!
I will follow you forever, cling to you through weal
   or woe!
Not so much the dread of going as the sundering
   of ties
That have bound us to our Eden, brought the tears
   into my eyes;
So I answer: Yes, my husband, yes, my darling,
   brave and true,
Go where judgment seems to lead you, I will
   surely go with you!
We will keep from out the shadows, gather sunshine where we may,
Hold our golden cup of being up for blessings
   every day!
Bear with patient resignation, all the gloomy evil
   days,
If our Father sends us any, ever giving Him the
   praise.
And our comfort in our children will be lustres to
   us then;
They will seem much nearer to our souls than ever
   they have been,
They will help us in our toiling, lighten every load
   they can,
They will both be cheerful workers, and HARRY's
   most a man.

There, besides, is dear old father, who will **go,**
  though hard 'twill be
To forsake his buried treasure down beneath the
  willow-tree.
So I look with hopeful pleasure to the coming of
  the day
That shall find us bravely journeying upon our
  westward way!"

PART SECOND.

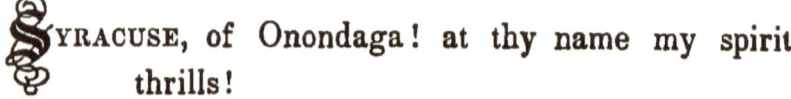

SYRACUSE, of Onondaga! at thy name my spirit
thrills!

And thy presence drifts before me, girt by thy ce-
rulean hills!

Every avenue and alley, every square and bridge,
and street

In thy dear old corporation is familiar to my feet!

I have strolled through all thy valleys, counted every
singing rill,

And have watched thy great heart beating, from
the crown of Prospect Hill.

All between thee and Salina, where thy crystal
treasures lay,*

I have wandered through the mazes of those acres
many a day;

---

* The great fields of salt vats.

Oh, I love to think upon thee, all these weary
years apart.
Syracuse! I send thee greeting! darling city of my
heart!
Call to thee from "Belle Missouri," from her rich
metallic hills,
From her broad luxuriant prairies, from her silver
threads of rills!
From her orchards and her vinyards and her "sheep-
besprinkled downs,"
From her rivers and her waterfalls, her cities and
her towns!
Oh, remember her brave people, who in battle's
bloody strife
Have proved that love of freedom far outweighs
their love of life!
See their ever glorious ballots, as I hold them to
the sun —
Every one a deed of valor in the cause of freedom done —
Oh, remember, how the nation echoed back the
sturdy blow
That consigned her demon, slavery, to its fitting
home below!
Oh, remember, too, her ruins — blazing homes and
wasted farms!
And the murders at her firesides and wild midnight
alarms!

Oh, those lonely, blackened chimneys shall be mon-
uments of pride!

Telling every coming stranger: "Here a Union
household died! —

Here for freedom's sake were suffered all the
woes that flesh can know,

Stabs and shots, and flames and curses, from a
drunken, brutal foe!

Here amid wild desolations some true hearts have
ceased to live!

Thus for Liberty and Union giving all that man
can give!"

Still, remember, "Belle Missouri" makes no murmur of regret;

Though all mangled, torn and bleeding she is not
disheartened yet!

Like a queen she rises proudly, calmly stern amid
her woes,

Binding up her bleeding temples she again confronts
her foes!

Thank God! her darkness brightens! all rebellion's
hosts elate,

Have been driven in confusion from out her lovely
State!

And now, in vales where lately fierce bloody deeds
were done,

Houses rise up from their ashes! fences glisten in
the sun!

Billowy fields of wheat are nodding joyously their
    heads of gold!
Scythes are singing in the meadows! plows are
    crunching in the mold!
Then cry: "Hail to Belle Missouri!" Syracuse, my
    early pride,
In the seven-times heated furnace has her loyalty
    been tried!
She has exorcised her demons, clothed in reason
    now she stands,
Proud and queenly, rich and lovely, State of states,
    and land of lands!
Yes, I love thee, Central City, as did RICHARD on
    that day
When, with all his dear ones round him, he was
    swiftly borne away —
Borne forever from the cottage where had passed his
    early days;
Sighing, as familiar places swiftly vanished from his
    gaze.
Sighing deeper, as he pondered, why, in this brief
    lease of life,
Man against his fellow-mortal should array himself
    in strife;
Why with malice and with vengeance man his
    brother should pursue,
When 'tis better to be gentle, kind and loving, good
    and true.

       *   *   *

Face to face with great Niagara RICHARD and his
household stand —

Awed to silence, lost in wonder, almost breathless,
hand in hand,

On the deck of the small steamer, gazing at the
giddy crown

Of that roaring, fearful deluge, spanned by rainbows, rushing down!

Spectacle to be remembered 'mid belittling things
of earth!

Ne'er will grander vision greet us till we know a
higher birth!

Several days did RICHARD linger, chained to that
enchanting spot,

Brimming all his soul with mem'ries never more to
be forgot.

Through the groves of Iris Island daily with his
dear ones strolled,

Dreaming out the grand old legends that the rushing waters told,

While the vast primeval cedars, spreading wide their
verdant arms,

Added coolness to the splendor of Niagara's varied
charms.

More contrite and meek in spirit, to his Maker closer
drawn

By the sermon of Niagara, RICHARD journeyed further on;

Paused a day to view Chicago, whose strange hist'ry
   bears the stamp
Of the wild tales of Alladdin and his genii haunted
   lamp.
Viewed with pride the interchanging, East with West,
   and man with man,
By the hundred handed railroads and the fleets of
   Michigan;
Viewed the palaces of marble in a long line white
   and new,
Catching the first rays of sunshine flung across the
   dancing blue;
Grew bewildered o'er discussions of the rise and
   fall of grain,
Corner lots, suburban ventures, river frontage, loss
   and gain,
And with all the vast importance of Chicago deep
   impressed
On the tablets of his spirit, he resumed his journey
   west.
Swiftly flying over bridges while the waters flashed
   beneath,
Turning bluffs and threading valleys on they rattled
   to Dunleith!
Where historic Mississippi, vast and deep and wide
   and bright,
In its silvery effulgence bursts in grandeur on the
   sight!

There was hurry of embarking, anxious fears for
trunks and freight,

Baggage heaped up in confusion, parcels crushed at
fearful rate,

Whistles screaming, bells aringing, runners drumming
for each boat,

Glad was RICHARD and his darlings when at last
they got afloat!

All was quiet on the river, brightly shone the stars
o'er head,

Puffing, puffing up the current, strongly on the
steamer sped.

Perched on piles of bales and boxes, interchanging
jests, the hands

Calmly wait the hurried labor when the steamer
"woods" or "lands."

"Light the torches!" "Throw the stage out!" "Who
can tell us where we are?"

"Bad-Axe Landing!" "Put that freight out!"
"Haul the stage in!" "Lively there!"

On again the steamer pushes, passengers again
subside,

Silence reigns throughout the cabin, all is still along
the tide.

With the first blush of the morning RICHARD's family
were out,

To behold historic places they might pass upon the
route.

Rafts of lumber, skiffs of Indians, towering bluffs,
 and islands green,
Towns and landings, boats and woodpiles were the
 main things to be seen.
Soon the sense of vision wearied — all the towns
 looked rude and small,
Till, upon her rocky terrace, they beheld and hailed
 St. Paul!
Here they purchased teams and wagons, over land
 pursued their way,
Pitching tents at early evening, moving on at break
 of day.
O'er the rushing Minnesota on a ferry they did
 ride,
Where the battlements of Snelling loom above the
 river side!
By the side of "Laughing Water" camped the first
 day from St. Paul,
Sweetly hushed to gentle slumber by the music of
 its fall.
Then they moved across the country — lovelier spots
 were never seen, —
Fairy-lakes and groves of timber, rolling prairies,
 fresh and green.
Then along Sauk River Valley, where the Scan-
 dinavian farms,
Rich with corn and wheat and barley, add a substance to the charms!

2

Where in grand old fire-places merry flames leap
    high and red,
When the winter's chilling mantle o'er the shivering
    earth is spread!
On they travelled up the valley — slowly journeyed
    day by day,
Passed Sauk Centre and Kandotta, paper cities, on
    their way.
Those were days when speculation's wild and crazy
    tide ran high —
Fools mapped cities by the thousand, luring other fools
    to buy!
But they failed to compass RICHARD, though their
    toils were nicely set;
Sternly following up a purpose — further on he
    travelled yet.
Where the lakes of Douglas County wide their liquid
    silver spread,
And clean groves of sugar-maples waved their grace-
    ful arms o'er head,
Where rich undulating prairies, fringed with timber,
    long had lain,
Pierced by streams and green with meadows, off'ring
    ready fields for grain.
Toward this fairy combination, steadily did RICHARD
    tend,
Where, at last, in glad fruition, his long journey had
    its end!

PART THIRD.

———◦◦———

FLOATING o'er the silvery waters of Lake Ida, clear
and strong,
On a bright autumnal morning came a wild entranc-
ing song.
'Twas a song of Indian legend, of a spirit ill at
rest,
Wandering in the land of shadows ever wretched and
unblest.
How the echoes flung the music back in chorus from
the shore.
As the singer beat the measures with the dipping of
her oar.
Swiftly, as a swallow gliding, toward the shore the
shallop sped,
Leaving rearward on the waters flashing lines of
silver thread!

19

Slender, graceful, was the figure, clad in semi-Indian
  dress,
And her Gallic, classic features   true ideal loveliness.
Rare and beautiful young being   in this wild, secluded
  spot,
Oh, whence come you? whither going? but the echoes
  answer not.
HARRY THORNTON, who was standing   with his rifle
  in his hand,
Gazed in wonder as the maiden lightly sprang out on
  the sand;
Gazed with senses all bewildered   as she moored
  her little boat,
Then a crowding swarm of queries through his puzzled
  brain did float:
"Surely, she was not an Indian?"   Ah, that sweet
  face answered "no!"
Yet her boat and strange apparel seemed to say: "It
  might be so!"
Round her neck she wore a collar from the grebe-
  duck's glossy skin,
And a scarlet woolen jacket kept her heaving bosom
  in;
Jacket trimmed with beads, and feathers from the
  great bald eagle's breast,
Thickly mingled with the plumage of the raven's
  purple crest.

Soft and white, her slim waist clasping, with its
 pendants hanging low,
Was a bead-bound graceful girdle, made from snowy
 cariboo.
Seals and charms and curious trinkets, formed from
 elk-horn, polished bright,
And carnelians, carved in figures, dangled in the
 morning light.
Then her skirt of dark blue broadcloth, dropping
 just below the knee,
Fringed with silk around the bottom, was as neat as
 neat could be.
Eyes so large and dark and thoughtful, oh, what
 glorious eyes were those —
Eyelids fringed with silken lashes, long and handsome
 in repose.
Oval features, cheeks of velvet, teeth as white as
 purest pearl,
Raven hair, and mouth as lovely as e'er graced a
 city girl.
Hands and feet! what tiny patterns of what hands
 and feet should be!
Captivating little Venus! goddess of an inland sea,
HARRY THORNTON's heart is leaping with a throb
 he 'll ne'er forget,
Through his soul there flows a longing! young love's
 tide has fairly set!

"Sir, good morning," spoke the maiden, frankly giv-
    ing him her hand,
" Father lives away up yonder, just behind that point
    of land.
All last night we saw your fires and this morn your
    white tents shine,
So I came to bid you welcome to this lovely lake
    of mine!
I have christened it Lake Ida, sister's name in mind
    to keep,
Who, beneath a balm of Gilead, sleeps that never
    ending sleep.
Father trades with the Ojibways, mother is Ojibway,
    too,
And my name, sir, is MANOMIN; pray, sir, tell me,
    who are you?
"I am simply HARRY THORNTON, those are father's
    tents you see;
We have all come here to settle, father, mother, sis,
    and me.
As the weary miles we traveled from a far off city
    here,
Little did we dream of finding such a sweet young
    neighbor near;
And when first I saw you coming, like a fairy from
    the skies,
Though my spirit drank your music, yet I could not
    trust my eyes!"

"Oh, sir, I am not a fairy — nothing but a half-breed
 girl —
And amid the tide of fashion, in a busy city's
 whirl,
When the blaze of regal beauty, loveliness refined,
 adorned,
Turned its splendors full upon me, ah your fairy
 would be scorned!
Here you see me 'mid surroundings rude and rough,
 uncouth and wild,
Clothed in all the rich profusion a fond father clothes
 his child,
And compare me with the Indian maids and matrons
 flitting by —
There I grant you, there's no fairy more a fairy here
 than I!
But before your blazing beauties I should vanish like
 the moon,
Who, when full, is bright at midnight, but is lost in
 light at noon!
Don't say nay, sir, what I tell you is the truth, you
 may depend,
Here, sir, I am free and happy, only longing for
 a friend,
Some congenial, kind companion that my heart might
 twine around,
Then I would not leave Lake Ida, e'en to be an
 empress crowned!

How I hoped that little sister would have lived, but
    all in vain;

She was but a ray from Heaven, soon she melted
    back again!

So I've come to see if you, sir, — oh, forgive, if I
    offend

By my frankness, — if, perhaps, sir, you would be
    MANOMIN's friend?

You, your father, mother, sister, all shall be dear
    friends of mine —

Oh, my spirit reaches to you like the tendrils of
    a vine!"

What a flood of blissful feeling rushed through HAR-
    RY's heart and brain!

Floods magnetic through his spirit throbbed as pulses
    throb with pain,

And he answered: "Yes, MANOMIN, gladly will I be
    your friend,

And God grant, that like a circle, this dear pledge
    may have no end!

Call me HARRY, treat me frankly, and how happy
    we shall be;

Come, MANOMIN, come to mother, all shall welcome
    you with me!

I will show you dear old grandpa, darling little
    JESSIE too,

They will join with me, MANOMIN, in this friendship's
    pledge with you!"

"Well, then wait a moment, HARRY, father sends a
    few wild geese,
I have also brought some wild rice, as an offering
    of peace.
In your tongue my name is "'Wild Rice,'" and in
    future, when you see
Wild rice all along our rivers, it may make you
    think of me."
"Think of you? can I forget you! From this mo-
    ment, I declare,
Through my spirit flows a river, wild rice growing
    ever there!
Stop, MANOMIN, let me carry that great pack of
    heavy things —
Is this queer thing a goose, MANOMIN? bodkin bill
    and speckled wings?"
"Goose? oh, no, sir! that is nothing but a *singebis*,
    or loon,
Which I shot while I was fishing at the inlet
    yester'noon!"
"What, you shot it?" "Yes, indeed, sir, don't you
    see my rifle here?
Many an elk has bowed before it, many and many
    a bear and deer."
Then she swung aloft her rifle, angry flashing in
    the sun:
"Here it is, sir! ah, you know not half the valiant
    deeds it's done!

Come, sometime, to father's cabin, you shall see a
    strange sight there, —
Trees festooned with fowl and ven'son, strips of elk,
    and steaks of bear;
Loon skins, of resplendent colors, fashioned into capes
    and hoods,
Cuffs and collars and fur wrappers, life crop of the
    lakes and woods!
Such the harvest which we gather, wild MANOMIN
    and her gun,
But for sport I never hunted, never killed a thing
    for fun;
Even wolves slink off in safety which offends my
    father sore,
Though I shoot them when they venture round the
    precincts of our door.
When I fish, for food I angle, when I hunt, for
    food I kill,
Often for a starving neighbor — which is more praise-
    worthy still.
Oh, improvident and wretched, steeped in vice, de-
    spair and woe,
Are our poor, unhappy Indians — but the whites
    have made them so!
Even father, darling father — he who loves me more
    than life,
Through the greed of traffic daily scatters wide the
    seeds of strife!

Oft with tears I have besought him to leave off his
    hurtful trade,

But he has not hearkened to me, ne'er will hearken,
    I 'm afraid!''

Thus they chatted, pure and simple, frank of heart,
    and good and true,

Naught of envious pride or hatred, naught of selfish-
    ness they knew.

All the world seemed full of glory, candor, honor,
    love and truth.

God! 'tis shameful the undreaming all our holy
    dreams of youth!

Presently they reached the campment, where, beneath
    a grateful shade,

Tents were pitched and fires builded and the daily
    meals were made.

Here MANOMIN's cordial welcome caused some truant
    tears to start,

But she hid them as she gathered little JESSIE to
    her heart.

We will leave her for the present, happy in her new-
    found friends,

Twining JESSIE'S sunny tresses 'round her tapering
    finger ends.

PART FOURTH.

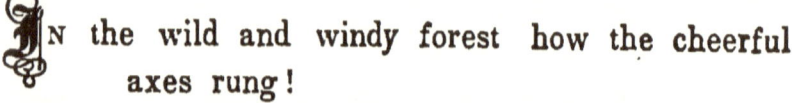

IN the wild and windy forest how the cheerful
axes rung!
While old Autumn on the choppers golden showers
thickly flung!
From the wrinkled limbs of lindens, from the spreading tops of elms,
From the tall and trembling aspens, piercing into
spirit realms,
From great oaks and balms of Gilead, that for centuries had stood,
From the silver plumaged maples, pride and beauty
of the wood,
From the button-wood and walnut and the ash-tree's
lofty crown,
From the iron-wood and willows swept the glittering
treasures down!

28

Axes rang and laughter bounded, while majestic
    over all
Rose the thunder of the timber, sweeping grandly
    to its fall!
All the settlers had assembled, sturdy, brown, broad-
    handed band,
With their axes on their shoulders, come to lend a
    helping hand
In the rearing of a dwelling for the stranger just
    arrived,
Vowing they would never leave him till his family
    were hived!
Chopping down and nicely hewing, smooth and thin,
    the forest trees,   .
Sawing, riving, shaving shingles, all were busier than
    bees!
Bossed by Uncle ANDREAS DARLING day by day the
    dwelling grew
'Neath that busy band of workers, while their jokes
    like arrows flew;
Trowels scraped and hammers rattled, axes glim-
    mered in the sun;
Roofed and plastered, floored and windowed, RICH-
    ARD'S house at last was done.
"Now then, boys," said Uncle DARLING, "many help-
    ers make work light,
Let us move in all this plunder, then we'll have a
    jig to-night!"

Chairs and tables, bales and boxes from the wagons
were unbound,

Beds put up and in the mean time two young men
were sent around

To invite the girls, and hire, if they could, old JIM
McBRIDE,

Who was a most splendid fiddler and a jolly chap
beside!

HARRY THORNTON and MANOMIN meanwhile hunted
far and near,

Trolled for trout and bass and pickerel, laid in wait
for bear and deer,

Visited cranberry-marshes, gathered wild plums and
wild pears,

Bagged fat pigeons by the dozen, caught young
partridges in snares.

Oh, the bliss of those excursions in MANOMIN's light
canoe!

Oh, the joys that thrilled their spirits as they tramped
those forests through!

Many a deer escaped their bullets, lost they many a
finny prize,

When, instead of "bobs" and "runways" they but
watched each other's eyes!

Yet, withal, they were successful, loads of fish they
daily caught,

Piles of game of different species — every evening
home they brought.

To have solved the question fairly might have
    eternized the name
Of the most sagacious lawyer, e'en of Philadelphian
    fame!
In a grove of sugar-maples ESTHER spread the re-
    past out.
What a sight for Epicurus, if that god had been
    about:
Blue-winged teals and royal mallards, fed upon wild
    celery beds,
Black ducks, marsh-hens, juicy widgeons, fat and
    savory crimson-heads,
Plump wild geese and golden pheasants, prairie
    chickens, young and sweet,
Richly dressed and brownly roasted, more than fifty
    men could eat!
Broad, black bass and mammoth pickerel, stuffed
    with highly seasoned paste,
Pike and trout, all poured with sauces, cooked to suit
    the daintiest taste,
Haunches of the tenderest ven'son, juicy sirloins of
    the bear,
Steaks of elk and steaming pot-pies filled with
    buttery grouse were there!
Berries stewed to crimson sauces, vegetables of every
    kind,
Flakey biscuit, golden butter — really, the bewildered
    mind

Shrinks from the enumeration of the many viands
    there,
Grows confused and lost in wonder at this princely
    bill of fare!
Praise was lavished on the hunters 'mid sly twinkles
    of the eye,
When MANOMIN, quickly rising, stole in silence,
    blushing, by;
HARRY also soon was missing, but the roaring feast
    went on,
Dishes rattled, glasses jingled, red with blood of
    demi-john!
Fragrant coffee poured its incense wide upon the
    star-lit air,
Savory smells of roasted dishes smote the senses
    everywhere!
Down along the loaded table colored lanterns hung
    in range,
Rendering the whole scene bewildering, oriental,
    wild and strange.
Surely, Ida's silvery echoes never were thus woke
    before,
Never answered back such music gaily ringing round
    her shore!
On the floor the couples gather, wild and free the
    music swells,
Round and round the brawny hunters twirl the hyper-
    borean belles!

How they danced, and how the music poured its
    volume of sweet sound,
How all flew when Uncle JIMMY called out loudly:
    "All hands round!"
Oh, it was a happy party, wild and joyous, full of
    glee,
All their hearts were running over, full of fun as
    hearts could be!
Uncle DARLING waltzed and polkaed, danced the
    schottish o'er and o'er,
Ending with the jig of juba hoed down *solus* on
    the floor!
Then the guests commenced departing and "good
    nights" were kindly said,
Though it should have been "good morning," as the
    east was getting red,
And, before the echoing laughter of the party died
    away,
Level beams of silvery sunshine registered a new-
    born day!
ESTHER, after briefly slumbering, bathed her face,
    and changed her gown,
Then, assisted by MANOMIN, went to work to "settle
    down."
Little JESSIE and her grand-pa still were sleeping
    over-head
In the yet unfinished chamber, on a temporary
    bed.

Long they'd watched the noisy frolic with a truly
    childish zest,
Age and youth, at last succumbing, wearied out they
    sought their rest.
How they slumbered, sweetly slumbered, — while the
    sun rose bright and high,
Pouring floods of glory earthward, through a cloud-
    less autumn-sky.
HARRY and his father early — scarcely seven by
    the clock, —
Went to felling stable-timber for the housing of their
    stock.
Ere they went the little table, nice and cosy, had
    been spread,
Glorious coffee, breast of chicken, yellow butter,
    snowy bread,
Were the items all sat down to — HARRY by MANO-
    MIN's side —
Glowing thoughts were his that morning — oh, their
    range was wild and wide!

Now, that ESTHER and MANOMIN had the field unto
    themselves
How they worked! They raised the cup-board, scour-
    ed and put up the shelves,
Washed the floors and cleaned the windows, tacked
    the front-room carpet down,

Moved in RICHARD'S walnut book-case, dusted clean
    from base to crown,
Hung, on cords before each window, nice white mus-
    lin curtains up,
Scoured basins, knives and sauce-pans, washed each
    plate and dish and cup,
Made the beds and hung the pictures and the mirror
    on the wall,
Nailed some hooks up for the rifles, also some for
    hat or shawl.
Out of chaos they brought order, and before the set
    of sun
They had finished up their labor all that they could
    do was done.
Snugly, in its cumbrous package, left to lie another
    day,
Waiting brawnier arms and sinews, mutely the piano
    lay.
Evening came, and all were gathered round the fire's
    cheerful light,
Once more happy and contented RICHARD'S heart
    brimmed with delight.
Worn and weary with their labor early all retired
    to bed,
JESSIE and MANOMIN going to the little room o'er-
    head.
Thus auspicious, rich with promise, opened RICHARD'S
    new career,

'Mid a host of cordial neighbors, on a prospering
frontier,
Blessed with health, and strength, and patience,
cheerful heart and willing hand,
Teams sufficient, and utensils, rich and fruitful vir-
gin land,
Snug and comfortable dwelling, stores enough to last
a year,
Wife and children, books and music, what had
RICHARD'S heart to fear?
Different dreams that night were HARRY'S: scarlet
waists and beads and quills,
Soft black eyes and thrilling kisses to the brim his
spirit fills!
Weary sleepers, slumber sweetly, we will bid you
a " good night " —
Undisturbed pursue your wand'rings through the
dream-land valleys bright.

'Twas the hazy Indian summer, sweetest period of
the year,
All the purple forests echoed with the bounding tread
of deer!
And the rippling, splashing noises of the water-fowl
at night
Filled the spirit of the Indian with the throbbings of
delight!

Everywhere the sound of rifles told of busy hunters
    out,
Every night the glare of fires told of Indians
    about!
And the timid ESTHER shivered as she saw those
    nightly gleams,
While memories of Wyoming ensanguined all her
    dreams!
'Twas in vain MANOMIN told her, " the Ojibways
    were all true,
That they would never raise their hands against
    the whites, she knew,"
For a long time she was fearful and would tremble
    every night,
Gather JESSIE closely to her if an Indian came
    in sight.
But at last she grew accustomed to their presence,
    more and more,
Losing all her nervous feelings, when they came
    about her door.
And soon she had a torrent of Ojibway life to stem,
For her piano proved to be great medicine to them,
And to every nook and corner of their Reservation
    flew
The fame of that strange " singing-box," till every In-
    dian knew,
And longed to see it, and they came, both sexes,
    old and young,

And for days MANOMIN kindly explained in their
own tongue,
All about the shining wonder, all about the glistening
keys,
All about the hidden spirit that sobbed out the har-
monies !

PART FIFTH.

—◆◇◆—

WINTER whitened o'er the country, bitter winds
    howled round the door,
Yet MANOMIN came as often down to RICHARD'S,
    as before.
Oh, the Saxon in her nature daily waged a bitter
    strife
With her low and rude surroundings, yearning for
    a higher life.
Like the never varying needle, turning always to
    the pole,
Ever so to RICHARD'S dwelling turned her young
    aspiring soul.
How she hungered how she thirsted for the light
    that books can give!
And within the sphere of music seemed another
    life to live!

39

There was still a deeper passion, in those yearnings
    of the heart,
In which love for HARRY THORNTON played no
    secondary part.
Many months, in all her flittings, through the forest,
    o'er the tide,
Hunting, fishing, pleasure seeking, HARRY had been
    by her side;
Wise and manly, honest hearted, pure, unselfish,
    good and kind,
He was deeply, and forever, in her heart of hearts
    enshrined.
Then she loved sweet little JESSIE with a passion
    almost wild,
While — ah, love's just compensation — she was wor-
    shipped by the child.
See their tresses intermingle, ebony with brightest
    gold,
While MANOMIN is relating all the wonders mani-
    fold
Of the grim and dark old forest and the fern-fields,
    and the brake,
And the lost loon's mournful legend, ever crying
    round the lake.
Bright with happiness and beauty, prone before the
    hearthstone's flames,
Hear her teaching little JESSIE musical Ojibway
    names:

" *Nepe,* darling, means the water, *waugh-bo* is the
   term for drink,

Muck-o-day-muskik-ah-waugh-bo, ah you laugh, now
   would you think

That long name was meant for coffee? *Washkiss* is
   the bounding deer,

Mushkose, elk — *pewaughbec,* iron — oh, you'll learn
   them, never fear.

Waughpose, rabbitt — *bungee,* little — *buckety* means
   thin, or poor,

Also signifies "'I 'm hungry,'" often heard about
   your door.

Shema, woman — *waubun,* morning — and *kiagago*
   means "'I 've none.'"

Waukiagan stands for dwelling — *boskiasegan* is a
   gun.

Nesseshin means "'you are pretty'" — listening HAR-
   RY here broke in —

" Let me tell you then, MANOMIN, — *Bungee shema,*
   nesseshin ! "

How she blushed, but still continued — " *Mukwa,*
   JESSIE, stands for bear,

Oc-kick, bucket, or a kettle — *popuin,* a stool, or
   chair.

Nitchie, means a friend or fellow — *nepoo,* kill, to die,
   or dead,

Do-do-shaboo stands for butter, and *buckwauzhigan*
   for bread,

Neca means a goose — *mondamin* singnifies the **wav-**
　　ing corn,
And *chee-no-din* is the zephyr playing on the lake
　　at morn,
Muck-o-day is rifle-powder — *weweep,* quickly — *um-*
　　ba, go,
Scoota-waughbo, dreadful whisky, — the poor Indian's
　　direst foe.
Oween-in-de-shyon, nitchie, is to say, "'whence come
　　you, friend ? ' "
Dibbe-nin-ge-gan, a circle, ring, or thing without an
　　end,
Sha-ki-ess-scoota-wan, JESSIE, seldom drawn so leng-
　　thy, means
Those mysterious things your matches; *musco-tassa-*
　　min is beans.
There, I 'll finish, for the present, for your brain
　　has got its fill,
Let me kiss you, little darling — you have kept so
　　nice and still ! "

Those were happy winter-hours — the old fiddler,
　　JIM McBRIDE,
As a better place for trapping also came there to
　　reside.
Snugly stored away in crannies of the jolly fellow's
　　brain

There were lots of queer old stories of dark forests,
glen and plain,
There were songs and tunes and riddles, there were
games of every sort,
That filled up those hyperborean days with merriment
and sport.

Quickly sped the merry winter, soft and warm the
south winds pour,
All at once, with smells of daisies, spring came,
singing at the door,
Came with warbling of the robins, came with bud-
dings of the trees,
Every foot-print marked with flowers, incense flung
on every breeze.
Out of all those days of softness, out of all those days
of bloom,
'Mid the fresh and virgin greenness, 'mid the delicate
perfume,
On MANOMIN dawned the morning of a sad and
bitter day —
Death had borne her Indian mother to his dusky
realms away!
Deep and bitter was her sorrow, lowly drooped her
graceful head,
In the wide and silent forest, all alone there with
her dead !

For her father was off trafficking two hundred miles,
  or more,
At Lake Hassar's lonely trading-post, and evergreen-
  girt shore.
Suddenly, and unexpected, was her mother called
  away,
Without warning her freed spirit left its tenement
  of clay!
All the day, prostrate with sorrow, how she mourned
  beside the bed,
Pouring forth endearing accents to the cold, unheed-
  ing dead!
All the day the robins whistled, all the day the blue-
  birds sung,
All the day with spring-time melodies the forests
  gaily rung;
But MANOMIN did not heed them, lifted not her
  drooping head,
Never once the silent cabin echoed back her cheerful
  tread!
In the silvery edge of evening the old trapper, JIM
  McBRIDE,
On his forest-beat returning, to the cabin turned
  aside.
And from him the startled neighborhood MANOMIN's
  sorrow learned
And toward her little dwelling scores of feet were
  quickly turned.

Oh, she found no lack of mourners, many a sympathizing heart
Strove to cheer her in her sorrow, or to share with
 her a part.
ESTHER wound her arms about her in one long and
 fond embrace,
And, then smoothing back her tresses kissed the tears
 from off her face.
Old JIM — the brown and brawny — poked his fist
 into his eye,
And, with bright drops on it shining, vowed he knew
 not how to cry.
RICHARD THORNTON, kindly taking both her hands
 within his own,
Spoke endearing words of comfort in a sympathizing
 tone :
" Dear MANOMIN be not fearful, oh take heart," he
 kindly said,
" Let your tears flow for the living, they are wasted
 on the dead !
Oh, the change from earth's probation to the spirit-
 life above
Is escaping from a darkness to a scene of light and
 love !
Our own home shall be your dwelling-place — oh, do
 not look so wild,
For, darling, we will be your parents and you shall
 be our child ! "

Gently, then, did HARRY lead her out beneath the
    budding trees,
That her fevered, throbbing temples might be billowed
    by the breeze,
Tenderly upon his bosom, while he drew her aching
    head,
From his spirit's inmost chamber soft and tremulous-
    ly said:
"Darling, let me sun thy sorrow with my spirits plead-
    ing, warm,
Let me fold thee up forever from the shadow and
    the storm!
Oh, I love thee, dear MANOMIN, shall my love be
    all in vain?
Fold it up within thy spirit, as the flowers do the
    rain!
Hush! thy mother does not need thy tears, for she
    has sweetly flown
To that summer-land of loving hearts that soon shall
    be our own.
Once within that world of glory what a joy will
    then be ours:
Throbbing on 'mid constellations — God's eternal gar-
    den-flowers, —
While his blessings, like a nectar, poured from many
    a golden cup,
Endless streams of bliss ecstatic, fill our thirsty spirits
    up!

Oh, MANOMIN, shed your sadness, for the world is
     full of song;
Every shining, circling season brings its melodies
     along:
There is music in the spring-time, when the mellow,
     tender breeze
Whispers greetings to the grasses in angelic sym-
     phonies;
There is music in the summer, in the gently falling
     rain,
As it beats its liquid measures softly on the window-
     pane;
There is music in the autumn, in the leaves that float
     about,
Sadly sighing, gently breathing their existence sweet-
     ly out;
There is music in the winter, in the softly falling
     snow,
Gentle, unobtrusive music, so delicious and so low.
Life, itself, is made of music: sweetest strains our
     spirits give;
Let us thank the God who made us, dear MANOMIN,
     that we live!"

PART SIXTH.

SABBATH ON THE FRONTIER—HARRY'S PHILOSOPHY AND NOBLE SENTIMENTS — GAFFER, OF THE HOLLOW.

—————◦◦◦—————

FROM the vines and clinging parasites and tops
    of all the trees
Glorious, regal, queenly summer flung her banners
    to the breeze !
And the clustering *convolvuli* robed the bald old cliffs
    in blue
And snowy white and pink and red, while beads of
    glistening dew—
Sweet tears upon the morning's face — hung flashing
    in the sun
As royally he mounted up, his daily race to run.
On Lake Ida's sun-lit surface, like white clouds
    upon the dawn,
Calmly, somnolently swinging, here and there were
    flocks of swan,

While upon the strands of timber edging round those
    prairie-seas
Beat in rippling waves, an incense, odorating every
    breeze.
'Twas a pensive Sabbath morning, every energy re-
    prest
Nature joined in consecrating the Creator's hour of
    rest.
For it seemed as if the noiseless wave, hushed bird,
    and softened ray,
Were expressive adumbrations of the humble, quiet
    way
She would have us toiling mortals, in a tranquil spirit,
    seek
To keep thee — shining child of God — thou first day
    of the week!
HARRY THORNTON, on a mossy bank, down by a
    purling brook,
That sweetly stole from out the lake, was deep buried
    in a book.
And MANOMIN, sweetly, silently, sat close beside him
    there,
Diademing with wild roses little JESSIE's golden
    hair.
For a time with what avidity his hungry spirit
    fed
On those burning words eternal, then presently he
    said:

"Oh, MANOMIN, I've been reading of the life that
    is to be,
Of a white-robed, glorious morning, soon to dawn on
    you and me,
Soon, I say, because probation, long, to some, although
    it seem,
When compared to life eternal is a transitory gleam!
And I feel, whene'er I ponder on the brilliant things
    in store
For each one of us poor mortals, on that ever vernal
    shore,
I could bear all earth's afflictions, go through life all
    blind and lorn,
Daily groping to God's altar, there to thank Him I
    was born!
But our minds, although immortal, are contracted
    finite things: —
As the sun o'erpowers vision with the splendor that
    it flings
So we sink in contemplation of the wondrous works
    we trace
To the Hand that sowed with planets all the azure
    fields of space!
Sad, indeed, I feel, MANOMIN, as I frequently re-
    flect,
On the mournful, dark condition of the masses, who
    neglect

To encourage the unfolding of those principles, that
    shine
So bright in this material life and in the life di-
    vine!
Oh, those reachings of the spirit after wisdom, truth,
    and love,
After that broad fellowship that binds the angel hearts
    above,
After knowledge of eternal space and deep and hid-
    den things,
After primates and first causes amid Nature's mystic
    springs,
Never, never should be smothered by the weight of
    selfish cares,
Never, never should be strangled by the growth of
    worldly tares.
Doubtless many a thrifty farmer yearly tills his fruit-
    ful land,
Never wondering how the harvest springs so ready to
    his hand;
Never wondering how or why it is when he has
    sown so spare,
Such a bountiful abundance for his sickle should be
    there!
With no longings of the spirit for immortal things
    divine,
With no thoughts above his bullocks, with no cares
    above his swine,

Darkly plodding on his journey till he sinks beneath
his years,
To be born a puling infant, in the glorious inner
spheres!
Oh, I recognize the duties and realities of life,
Realize its heavy burdens, know the sharpness of its
strife,
Still, amid its toil and trouble, 'mid its anxious care
and pain,
I would garner up a treasure that should be eternal
gain!
Not of gold, and not of silver, houses, lands, or
costly gems,
But of love, and light, and knowledge, Heaven's
radiant diadems!
Years of enervating study, weary miles of travel,
sore,
Will not serve as *open sesames* to Nature's hidden
door.
'Tis a door that swingeth lightly, without chain, or
bar, or lock,
'Tis a door that opens freely to the humblest, if
they knock!
While the manly dew of labor gathers thick upon
my brow,
As I fell the heavy forest-trees, or tramp behind
the plow,

Every chip, or leaf, or flower, every shrub, or bush,
    or tree,
Every sod I turn or blade of grass speaks lovingly
    to me!
In the self same earth embedded, nourished by the
    self same rain,
Side by side the elm and maple, side by side the chess
    and grain,
Side by side a thousand natures, widely varying,
    daily grow,
Some maturing very quickly, some unfolding very
    slow,
Never mingling in confusion, but from earth and
    air and sun
How precisely the right principles are gathered to
    each one!
Thus I daily learn the lessons taught by flower and
    tree and sod,
While my glory-laden spirit beats in harmony with
    God!
Bows before the great Omnicient, Omnipresent, All
    in All,
In the ocean of whose bosom worlds unnumbered
    rise and fall!
Out of whose magnetic spirit every tree-leaf is un-
    rolled,
By whose love the eves of heaven are all fillagreed
    with gold!

By whose power the sap beats steady through the
veins of every tree,

By whose will the winds are driven over forest, plain,
and sea;

By whose sufferance the lightnings draw their gleaming sabers out,

By whose guidance every comet keeps its strange
erratic route!

Not the smallest microscopic animalculum that lives

Ever moves without the power that the great All-
father gives!

From His lovely life the flowers catch their thousand-
tinted hues!

From His bosom to the grasses flow the sweet, refreshing dews!

Every dream of immortality with which our minds
are rife,

Every law that guides our dear ones in the higher,
inner life,

All things in space that go to make the Grand
Eternal Whole

Assure me that each living thing lives in the Father's Soul!

We are richly blessed, MANOMIN, waked to being
'neath a sun

Where the blessed boon of freedom is conferred on
every one!

Every one! oh, God forgive me, I forgot the menial
    black,
With his groans and tears and manacles, and gashes
    on his back!
I forgot the sobbing children, clinging to their father's
    knees,
As at sight of the slave-trader all their young life's
    currents freeze,
I forgot the frantic mother, shrieking like a maniac
    wild,
As from out her bosom, ruthlessly, was torn her infant
    child!
Oh, I pity them, MANOMIN, but the time shall surely
    be
When God's bare arm from Heaven shall reach down
    and set them free!
What if through our fields deserted, crimsoned wide
    by war's red wave,
Over smoking homes just Heaven makes a pathway
    for the slave!
What if grief and death and terror, famine, pesti-
    lence and woe,
Through our land with desolations, pave a way for
    them to go!
What if you and I, MANOMIN, in that fearful reck-
    oning time,
Come to grief with other thousands innocent of this
    foul crime?

Could we blame our common Father, at whose feet
the groans and tears
Of this race have begged deliverance for a hundred
weary years?
Are they not as much his children as the whitest race
of men?
And from chains and lusts and beatings shall he not
release them then?
Oh, MANOMIN, our republic must yet lay aside this
sin!
She must rise and cast it from her as an adder casts
its skin!
Then redeemed! regenerated! founded on true freedom's rock!
She may face all allied powers, never trembling at
the shock!
And as luminous as God's great seal, set on the deed
of day,
Down the shining path of ages she may grandly
keep her way!
A Freedom's star of Bethlehem! — a bright beacon,
blazing clear!
Telling all the shipwrecked of the earth, '"sweet
freedom's port is here!"'
Yes, I say again, MANOMIN, we are blessed beyond
our ken,
That our day is made so glorious by the deeds of
glorious men!

Glorious in their Christian virtues, brightest jewels
of a state!
Glorious in their *academia*, which the world may
imitate,
Glorious in their clanging presses, scattering wisdom
far and wide,
Dropping papers, books and pamphlets at the farthest fireside!
Glorious in their independence and their simple
polity,
Glorious in their pride of labor, and their gentle
comity,
Glorious in their friendly feelings, holding out in-
viting hands
To oppression's struggling victims in the trans-Atlan-
tic lands!
Oh, my beating heart is swelling with a wild, immortal joy!
And I bless my God, MANOMIN, that I am a Yankee-
boy!"
"Yes, but HARRY, oh, how little know I of those
glorious things,
I am daughter of the forest where dark shadows
spread their wings!
True, the kind Great Spirit gave me a white father,
fond and good,
Then yourself, to shine upon me like a sun-beam
through the wood!

But my proud, ambitious spirit, struggling in this
    hybride clay,
Vainly plucks at clouds that gather and obscure its
    perfect day!
Though I've always yearned for wisdom litttle pro-
    gress still I made,
Till you came, for darling father thinks of nothing
    but his trade!
He would not have taught me, HARRY, of the glory
    of the spheres,
Where no bended form or wrinkles mark the wear
    and tear of years!
Nor have told me of the millions — millions upon
    millions more —
Bright, seraphic, happy beings, living on that shining
    shore!
You have made my heart a garden, where against
    love's arches shine
Hopes immortal, burst in blossom, fanned by atmo-
    spheres divine!
Oh, the future shines before us, all the countless
    coming years,
With a grandeur of God's smiling that so overflows
    the spheres!
Where, among celestial gardens, crowns of flowers
    ever bloom
For the brows of new immortals daily issuing from
    the tomb!

Often has my spirit wandered, in my wild ecstatic
    dreams,
Through that land of regnant summer, by the clear,
    immortal streams,
Where the roses bloom forever and forever, loved
    and blest,
Even poor, misguided Indians find an everlasting
    rest! —"
Here a sigh escaping near her made MANOMIN turn
    her head,
" Why! good GAFFER! how you frightened me!" she
    tremulously said.
" Fear not, daughter, peace be with you, for I bring
    you words of love;
You are bidden to my cabin by the shining ones
    above.
With you, too, my youthful brother, there be those
    that fain would speak,
Come with her and learn together what your eager
    spirits seek!
Come this evening, come to-morrow, or on any other
    day;
I am GAFFER of the Hollow, and MANOMIN knows
    the way!"
Saying which he wrapped his blanket closer round
    his slender frame
And departed through the undergrowth as strangely
    as he came.

PART SEVENTH.

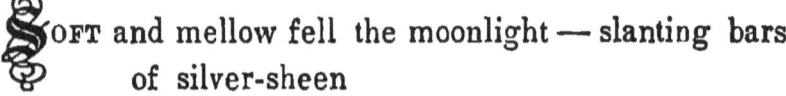

OFT and mellow fell the moonlight — slanting bars
 of silver-sheen
Flecked the forest with a brightness, piercing through
 the roof of green.
Deep, profoundest calm was reigning — slumber-
 locked seemed every breeze,
Loons were wailing in the marshes, glow-worms flaming 'mong the trees!
Like a lake of molten silver Ida lay beneath the
 light,
Flashing back the mirrored graces of bewitching sweet
 young Night!
In a graceful semi-circle swept the beach of glittering
 sand,
Where MANOMIN's skiff was lying, drawn half-way
 upon the strand.

60

What an atmosphere for lovers, everything conspired
to charm ;
Even forest-shadows wandered two by two and arm
in arm!
Slowly HARRY and MANOMIN moved along toward
the beach,
Tender, low, and deeply earnest, fell the music of
their speech.
They were talking of the future and comparing hopes
and fears,
Interchanging vows and pledges, laying plans for
coming years.
Castle building! sweet withdrawal from real life's
bewildering din!
Though of millions who build castles few there be
that enter in!
At the beach our lovers halted to decide which way
to take,
They were setting out for GAFFER'S — should they
go by shore or lake?
"Let us take the skiff, MANOMIN, I can row you
there, you know,
You will get so tired, darling, if the forest-path we
go.
Mother says that you have labored hard and faith-
fully all day,
So I think that we had better take the easiest,
shortest way."

"Oh, no, HARRY, 'twould be cruel! all day long you've held the plow,

And your arms, though strong and willing, must be weary even now;

Though I know, 'tis very pleasant in the skiff with you to ride,

Still, I think it will be nicer — arm in arm and side by side,

Through this flood of lunar glory, tinted by the forests green,

For us both to walk, my HARRY, and enjoy this glorious scene."

" Well, my darling, I am willing, even so then let it be ;

Oh, to feel you ever near me is sufficient joy for me."

So they journeyed on together, underneath the emerald boughs,

Living only in each other, breathing love, exchanging vows.

There were few in all that country — trader, trapper, warrior bold,

Child or woman, white or Indian — who with truth, might not have told

Strangest stories of this GAFFER, things experienced or heard —

Still 'twas rare to hear him mentioned, strangers
    never heard a word
Of the supernatural doings, day and night and night
    and day
At his cabin, in the hollow, wrought by spirits passed
    away.
'Twas a subject all avoided, none could read the riddle
    through —
To your questions they would answer: " I don't know,
    no more than you!
All I know, is, I have seen them, felt their hands,
    and heard them play
On the banjo, horn and fiddle, heard them come and
    go away!
Where they went to — where they came from — who
    they are I cannot tell,
There's the way to GAFFER'S cabin, try the thing
    yourself a spell! "
Perfect in its isolation GAFFER'S cabin darkly stood,
Girdled round by quaking aspens, in a hollow of the
    wood.
Grape-vines wove a woof above it, turning every ray
    of light,
Not a moon-beam crossed the threshold even on the
    brightest night.
The interior of the cabin was most primitive and
    rough,

That no juggler's art was practised here was evident
enough.

One large square room of hewn oak logs with no floor
except the earth,

A heavy table, fire - place, a single "bunk," or
"berth,"

An air-pump and a curious, rude electrical machine,

With some crucibles and blow-pipe in one corner
might be seen,

Three shelves of books, a violin, and banjo 'gainst
the wall,

A rifle and a microscope, a horn, and that was all,

Excepting some three-legged stools, and antlers of a
deer,

All other "helps" of jugglers were clearly wanting
here.

GAFFER, HARRY and MANOMIN, round the table
joined their hands.

Poor MANOMIN's heart went thumping up against her
bodice-bands;

Frightened, though she knew not wherefore, daring
not to speak a word,

How the cold chills rippled o'er her when some little
raps were heard!

Falling first so soft and gently, now they ceased, then
came again,

Thicker, faster, how they rattled, like the pattering
feet of rain!

Then a strong and heavy knocking, like a war-club's
    sonorous sound,
Rang three times upon the table, then smote dully on
    the ground !
Instantly the darkness vanished, fled before a brilliant
    gleam
Of a phosphorescent brightness, making poor MANO-
    MIN scream.
" Peace, my child, no danger threatens, oh, fear not,"
    a soft voice said ;
Then a white hand formed above her and descend-
    ing, stroked her head !
In a moment more it melted — through the room then
    moved a breeze,
Quickly followed by a moaning, like the moaning
    sound of seas;
On the banjo now an air was played upon a single
    string,
While a chorus of sweet voices sang as only angels
    sing !
Then the yellow gleam grew brighter, rose, and
    spread, and grew more bright,
Till no space was left for shadows — all the cabin
    glowed with light !
From the midst of which, a presence, bright. and
    beautiful and mild,
Gazed in love upon MANOMIN — oh, the mother
    sought her child !

5

Sought her child — what mother would not? Rest
assured, the law of love
Is the gravitation bringing all our dear ones from
above!
If the ether-ushered spirit's free to go where'er it
choose
Then to linger round its loved ones, what fond parent
could refuse?
"Oh, MANOMIN, fear no evil," spoke the presence
sweet and low,
"Love, instead, and peace and knowledge bring we
to our friends below!
I can scarcely find expression for the things I wish
to say,
Oh, so different lives the spirit, freed from its dark
bonds of clay!
We are like to persons calling unto one down in
a well:
Of the glories of the heavens and the landscapes
we would tell,
With the majesty of ocean, as its billows grandly
roll,
And sublimity of mountains we would fill his darkened soul.
We would tell him of the valleys and the far off
peopled stars,
Of cascades and brooks and rivers and the rainbow's
sun-dyed bars!

Of the forests and the prairies and the fields of
    waving grain,
Of the grasses, birds and flowers, of the falling dew
    and rain;
But he shuts his ears against us, saying: "'Cease
    this talk to me,
I have eyes and will and reason, but these things
    I cannot see!
Long and hollow is the landscape, circumscribed your
    spreading sky,
And I have no faith in mountains, nor in rainbows,
    no, not I!
I know all about the ocean, but its billows do not
    roll,
Birds and flowers are children's stories, they exist
    not in my soul!
Rocks and mosses are around me, overhead I see
    the sky;
Oh, your humbugs don't confound me, by my truths
    I'll live and die!'"
Pitying him, we slowly lower down a rope and draw
    him out,
Speech could not depict his feelings as his eyes sweep
    round about, —
"'Oh, the beauty, oh, the glory! to my vision here
    unrolled —
God forgive my doubts when truly not a millionth
    part was told!'"

So it is with you, my daughter: you may doubt the
    truths we tell,
For your spirit, too, is groping in the bottom of a well!
So was mine — oh, darkly groping — till, at length,
    you know that night —
A magnetic cord was lowered, — I was drawn up
    in the light!
And such light! oh, darling daughter, mind of man
    cannot conceive;
Every shrub and weed is radiant past your powers
    to believe!
While we move among the forests all their essences
    we see,
And the wonderful processes by which nature builds
    each tree!
Note the sugar seek the maple, see the resin seek
    the pine,
Watch the primates as they gather to the tree, the
    stalk or vine!
Mountain mosses, rocks and pebbles, stalk and grass,
    and flower and weed,
Ores and salts, as well as diamonds, insects, fruits,
    and roots and seed,
Houses, furniture and volumes, birds and animals,
    and man,
All are given different lustres in the great creative
    plan!
All the treasures of the ocean easily we can explore,

See its pearls and diamonds glitter on its ribbed and
rocky floor!
Down its wide and watery valleys note the endless
saurian swarms,
See the sea-plants widely reaching forth their hydro-
genous arms!
Every pulse within your body, every thought your
mind unfolds
Is as patent to our vision as the water ocean holds!
We know nothing here of darkness, shadows dwell
not where we are,
Space is one vast blaze of beauty, hither, thither,
near or far!
Round among the constellations we may freely flash
along,
Swelling the eternal chorus — Father God's harmonial
song!
By our widened, deepened vision, by our brighter,
higher birth,
We would pray you let your longings rise above the
things of earth!
Man is an eternal spirit, fruit of a creative love
Broader, deeper, far more boundless than your firm-
ament above!
Not to strive for place and power, not to hunger
for renown,
Not to buy and sell a brother, not to tread each
other down,

Not to heap up idle riches, not to grasp, with greedy
    hands,
Bonds and deeds and obligations, broad domains of
    idle lands,
Not to laden his bright spirit down with things of
    · little worth,
But to love, to live and let live, was man sent upon
    the earth!
Endless circles of progression, starting at the earth,
    flow on,
In which mill of life the spirit ever is refined upon!
Every trial, every hardship — when God's plan is
    understood,
Will be seen to be an agent for the working out
    of good!
Some experiences await you, and your mate there,
    by your side,
Which, though pregnant with sad heartaches, cannot
    well be turned aside!
As the forest-tree is strenghtened by the rude and
    ruthless blast,
So your spirits shall be stronger when your coming
    woes are past!
I shall hover ever near you, whispering hope when
    hope is low,
Good night, children, duties call me, all my blessings
    I bestow!"

PART EIGHTH.

MORE OF HARRY'S PHILOSOPHY — RICHARD'S ENEMY.

———◦∘◦———

IDA'S forest stood in beauty on that calm, mid-
    summer night,
Emerald foliage bathed in glorious, golden seas of
    lunar light,
Air as soft as breath of roses, nature's voices whisper-
    ing low,
O'er the silvery water's surface shadows flitted to
    and fro!
HARRY THORNTON and MANOMIN, in the moon-light,
    side by side,
Sat together, with their bare feet glistening in the
    cooling tide!
Innocent and pure in spirit, happy, guileless, loving
    pair!
E'en misanthrope might have loved them as they sat
    together there!

71

All the day along the furrow, with hot feet and
    dripping brow,
Patiently had HARRY THORNTON toiled behind the
    breaking plow!
And MANOMIN, ever present, back and forth, from
    morn till night,
Walking with him, talking with him, made his weary
    task seem light!
Little sunny-headed JESSIE, too, was with them all
    the day;
Sometimes with sweet-williams making the near ox's
    head look gay,
Sometimes slumbering in the shadow of a jack-oak,
    thick and low,
Sometimes butterflies pursuing, as they flitted to and
    fro,
Sometimes like a sunbeam darting 'neath the trees,
    whene'er she heard
The vivacious squirrel barking, or the whistle of a
    bird;
Sometimes in the furrow stalking with droll mimicry
    of tread,
Till MANOMIN caught and kissed her — darling little
    sunny-head!
As I said, the weary labor of the sultry day was
    done,
In the west there still was lingering some bright
    foot-prints of the sun,

While the moon came circling queenly o'er a roof
of forest green,
Robing HARRY and MANOMIN in a costly silver
sheen!
"How the wish is rising, HARRY, that I might be
rich and fair,
Learned and graceful as the ladies in those far off
cities are!
Then I'd buy a little cottage on some quiet river's
shore
Where we all would dwell together, you should never
labor more!
Do you know that every Indian looks with most
supreme disdain
On the toiling, sweating paleface, slaving 'mong his
roots and grain?"
"Yes, MANOMIN, well I know it — 'tis the curse of
that dark race,
For the rosary God blesses is the beads on labor's
face!
Not to labor is to perish, rust and mold, stagnate
and die!
'Tis to be the only idle thing of God's beneath the
sky!
Oh MANOMIN, all is labor through the universe of
God,
From the swinging of a planet to the breathing of
a sod!

How the restless sea is toiling, and the stars are
    beating loud,
And across the waste of heaven flies a lone, un-
    quiet cloud.
Toiling seasons sweep along the earth, winds shake
    the slumbrous flowers,
Bright lightnings fly and rains come down in frantic,
    sobbing showers!
The burning sun swift speeds along the western track
    of heaven,
Pursuing night comes flying up the eastern one
    at even!
Thus Nature's daily toil goes on forever round the
    world,
No rest for earth, no quiet cove where she with
    sails all furled
Might sweetly swing so tranquilly upon the heaving
    breast
Of God's eternal, endless deep, like a sleeping swan
    at rest!
Oh, the yearly builded structures of the birds in every
    tree,
And the ant's industrial lessons are God's sermons
    unto me!
Labor, labor is their burden, toil from dewy morn
    till night,
If you would be blessed and happy, if you would be
    strong and bright,

Labor, labor without ceasing, idleness begetteth crime,
Laboring nations are the grandest, in whatever age
 or clime!
Year on year the ancient adage proves itself to be
 most true:
Satan surely will find mischief for each idle hand
 to do!
But, MANOMIN, see how nearly the round moon hangs
 over head,
'Tis the noon of night, my darling, we must hasten
 off to bed!
For the cool, refreshing, dewy lips of early morning's
 light
Ought to kiss us in the furrow, — so, sweet moon and
 stars, good night!"

RICHARD THORNTON's life was flowing peaceful as
 a sunny dream
Wandering through the vales of slumber, like a broad
 and quiet stream.
Health and peace and bounteous plenty, merry hearts
 and sunny looks,
Toil, all silver-edged with music, precious hours with
 his books,
Were the blessings that had settled sweetly down
 within his breast,
Filling all his thankful being up with fullest sense
 of rest!

But how oft from unseen *nimbi* bursts an unexpected
    storm,

So defiantly ignoring the fair promises of morn!

One calm evening, while the sunset tinged with gold
    the growing grain,

Slowly o'er the rolling prairie came a solitary wain.

Drawn by bony, brindle oxen, poor and dismal look-
    ing things,

And the wagon cover painted blacker than Appolyon's
    wings!

Clad in heavy, grimy ducking, armed with sharp re-
    lentless goad,

Fierce, repelling, hairy creature seemed the owner
    of the load.

Not a note of childhood's laughter, not a gleam of
    woman's smile,

Not a flutter of a ribbon once relieved that dismal
    pile!

Silent, gloomy heap of blackness, hail ye from some
    demon's lair?

One would almost, 'neath the wagon, look to find
    cerberus there!

It was mail-day and the settlers, gathered in an idle
    throng,

Gazed intently on the stranger coming leisurely
    along.

Rough and various the conjectures as to whom the
    man might be

As he slowly came still nearer, like some great, dark
  destiny.

But they met him with a cordial grasp of hand and
  beam of eye,

Asked the news and if the crossings of the Sauk
  were getting dry?

How he liked the corduroying in the woods, which
  they had done?

Would he take a claim among them or still further
  travel on?

At that moment, RICHARD THORNTON, having just received his mail,

Stepped up briskly to the talkers, but his cheeks
  turned deadly pale

As he cast upon the stranger one quick look of wild
  alarm,

And prepared to hasten homeward, when a hand com-
  pressed his arm.

Quickly turning with a frightful, ashen pallor on
  his cheek,

Pulseless, tongue-tied for a moment he could scarcely move or speak.

But 'twas Uncle ANDREAS DARLING'S calm and pleasant eyes he met,

And a smile of reassurance gleamed among the drops
  of sweat

That in his great apprehension had bedewed his
  ruddy face —

"Hold on, THORNTON! where in blazes are you rushing at that pace?"

"Ha! good evening Uncle DARLING!" quickly giving him his hand,

"What's the news among the settlers? Have they
found old TOM LE GRAND?"

"No, poor fellow, he's a goner — ginseng's been the
death of him —

Five days lost — starved dead by this time — how
comes on old Uncle JIM?"

"Brisk as ever — full of music — he's a rare old
bit of clay —

He and HARRY and MANOMIN went out hunting
yesterday;

Away round the head of Carlos where that run'way
is, you know:

JIM and HARRY killed a bruin and MANOMIN shot
a doe;

So we've got a world of cutlets, steaks and roasts,
and fries and stews;

Come on over, Uncle DARLING, smoke your pipe and
read the news."

"Nothing, sure, would please me better, that I need
not tell you, DICK,

But I've got to do the milking, as my gals have
taken sick —

Raspberry shortcake's what's the matter — mother
crams in too much cream,

And the pesky stuff has laid 'em flatter than a
    puncheon beam!"
" Well, good night, then, I must hasten, for you see,
    'tis getting late;
ESTHER'll worry if the sun-down does not find me
    at the gate."
So they parted, RICHARD THORNTON hurrying with
    redoubled tread,
In his heart a wild foreboding of some great, impend-
    ing dread.
" God of mercy, God of justice, is there no where
    that I can
Hide me from the hideous presence of this base,
    revengeful man?
Dear as was our little cottage, and our friendships
    dearer still,
Yet we left them, vainly thinking to escape this man's
    ill will.
By what methods he will wrong me God in heaven
    only knows,
But the knowledge of his presence rings the knell
    of our repose!
Darling ESTHER, angel ESTHER, tender mother, lov-
    ing wife,
You have merited a smoother, greener, lovelier path
    of life!"
Such the anguishing reflections RICHARD'S mind con-
    ned o'er and o'er,

Ending only as his footfall crossed the threshold of
    his door.
There the cheerful scene that met him caused the
    shadows to depart,
Light his eyes with pleasure's beacons, cast the dem-
    ons from his heart.
On the hearth a cheerful fire sunned the chill from
    evening's air,
While old JIM, forever happy, puffed his pipe in
    comfort there.
In one corner ESTHER's father, o'er the Bible bend-
    ing low,
Read of that celestial city where his spirit longed
    to go.
And the table's snowy cover, gemmed with ware so
    pure and white,
And the odorous smells of coffee, filled his senses
    with delight.
Sure, it needed not that ESTHER should entwine him
    in her arms,
Or have kissed his lips so fondly, to have banished
    his alarms.
Yet, the loving creature did it, and I am not sure
    but he
Gave her back those self-same kisses, as he drew her
    on his knee.
Then as JESSIE and MANOMIN played some old and
    simple tunes

Through his spirit flowed the sweetness of a thousand
  gathered Junes!
And that night while all were sleeping, quietly,
  without a fear,
To his wife he turned and whispered: "ESTHER,
  ROBERT KING IS HERE!"

ROBERT KING'S CABIN — UNCLE DARLING AND "BITING BETTY" — "BITING BETTY" MARKS A STRAY!

—•◦•—

WHERE the dark primeval forest skirted Ida's
    eastern face
ROBERT KING had built his cabin, in a most secluded
    place.
No bright glimpses of the water, or the shell-be-
    jewelled shore,
Or the sweetly meaded prairie fondly met you at
    his door! ·
For his cabin, small and wretched, in a gloomy hol-
    low stood,
Made obscurer by the debris of the patriarchal wood!
And a sudden, firm conviction that this wretch, so
    hid away,
Was a scheming villain, skulking from the honest
    light of day,

82

Forced itself at once upon you when his dwelling
    met your eyes,
And a hot, repulsive feeling in your breast would
    quickly rise.
From all friendly calls and visits in immunity he
    dwelt,
Not a neighbor's heart toward him a kindly impulse
    felt.
For shamefully and scornfully, to every one's amaze,
He'd slighted all the offers made to come and help
    him raise.
And with but simply slighting them he did not rest
    content,
But to Uncle ANDREAS DARLING an insulting note
    he sent,
And the tenor of the billet was, that every one must
    mind
Their own concerns more strictly, or they would
    surely find
That they had kindled needlessly a bitter, hostile
    flame,
For he would not suffer meddling, under any form or
    name!
Uncle DARLING read the missive with a wondering
    surprise,
Then a flash of indignation gleamed a moment from
    his eyes,

And he took down " Biting Betty " from the hooks
just o'er his bed,

And dosed her with a powder, then a sugar plum of
lead,

And while settling her stomach thus he quietly did
say :

" Old Bet, I give you warning now to keep out of
that chap's way !

Because, through all the settlement you can't deny,
'tis known

That you have got a hasty, fiery temper of your
own,

And if at that old hedghog you should, some time,
let fling,

Why, you see as how old Betty 'twould be bad for
ROBERT KING !

But now, old Bet, my darling, let us mosey up the
lakes,

To wake up those young goslings that sleep among
the brakes,

And if, by any accident, we meet this critter now,

For goodness sake old Betty, don't get me in a row ! "

So he shouldered her and started through the woods,
and far away,

Crossed the marshes and the hollows and climbed
the cliffs so gray,

And never checked his footsteps till he reached the
gloomy glade

Where the wretch of his soliloquy his dreary h
    had made!
As he passed the silent cabin not a stir of life was
    there
But the dismal wagon-cover, swinging wildly in the
    air;
Not a single bird chirped cheerily to break the still-
    ness round,
And "wolf" was all the "varmint sign" he found
    upon the ground!
On he strode through groves of poplar and great fields
    of prickly ash,
Never heeding rents or scratches, or sometimes a
    deeper gash,
Presently he reached a hollow skirting RICHARD
    THORNTON's claim,
Where a lovely grape-vine arbor bore sweet little
    JESSIE's name.
Here he paused, for sounds of voices touched his
    ever listening ear,
And he hid himself a moment, wondering who was
    drawing near.
It was JESSIE, and her mother who were slowly
    coming there,
Talking, singing, telling stories, walking out to take
    the air.
Briskly stepping from his cover, with his smiling
    eyes alight,

He was going on to meet them when a man's form
    came in sight.
Back again behind his shelter, stepping light as
    sylvan elf,
"Ha!" he whispered, "by old Goshen! there's that
    'tarnal KING himself!"
So it was, and ESTHER saw him and endeavored to
    turn back,
But all grim, his hated presence stretched itself
    across her track;
Gathering all her strength together she prepared her-
    self to hear
Taunts and insults and dark threatenings, as the
    dreaded man drew near.
"Ah, Miss ESTHER — Missis THORNTON! — so you
    fled to hide from me!
That's a job, my whilome sweetheart, not so easy
    done, you see!
As the hound, though slowly tracking, finds at last
    the flying deer,
So from point to point I traced you, till at length I
    found you here!
Here I'm watching, here I'm waiting, you shall
    never know relief,
Soon, again, I warn you, madam, you and yours
    shall come to grief!
Well you know my vow that evening that you stabbed
    me with your scorn,

That I'd wring your heart until you cursed the day
that you were born!

Years and years your joys enraged me — years so
bitter, gaunt and grim —

Oh, I could have eat my heart out in my hate of
you and him!

But you know the sequel, ESTHER — here's that cottage deed, my dear!

That same thing shall be repeated — you shall soon
be homeless here!

Yet, I think, on one condition I would bid my vengeance cease,

And abandon plans maturing, soon to wreck your
present peace!

You are young, and fresh yet, ESTHER, see the bloom
upon your cheek,

Come, and feed me on its roses in my cabin once
a week!

Now there is a " — " Silence, villain, stand aside, sir,
from my path!

You have got a tongue more devilish than the blackest
demon hath!

Stand aside, sir, scheming coward, base insulting,
wicked thing,

I despise your foolish threatenings as I scorn *you,*
ROBERT KING!"

"Nay, now calm your ruffled feathers, smooth your
plumage, pretty bird;

I can force you if I choose to, for your screams cannot
     be heard."
And he laid his hand upon her; at that instant,
     loud and clear,
Rang the tone of DARLING'S rifle, and a bullet smote
     his ear.
Stunned and bleeding, back he staggered, nearly fall-
     ing to the ground,
And the offending hand was quickly pressed upon
     the painful wound.
Uncle DARLING paused a moment, just a moment to
     reload,
And to cap "Old Biting Betty," forward then he
     quickly strode,
Heeding not KING's leveled rifle with its rampant
     hammer grim,
Heeding not his burning eyeballs, but with eyes fixed
     straight on him,
Swiftly up he rushed and caught him, struck the rifle
     from his hand,
Then confronted and addressed him in provoking
     accents bland:
"Really stranger you'll excuse me, but you see,
     I kinder thought,
That yer weap'n was a pintin, jest now whar it hadn't
     ought.
May be 'twas because my eyesight aint so good as 't
     use to be.

But I swow now I felt sartin you was pokin her
    at me!"
"So I was, and I intended to have shot you through
    the head!
I can only thank your blindness that I'm not among
    the dead!"
"Wall, it is a pity, stranger—yet I *kin* see middlin
    clear—
Anyhow, I'll bet a mink-skin, that I popped you
    through the ear!
No use getting riley, stranger—case with me that
    never pays—
Ear-holes is the mark "Old Betty" allers puts upon
    my strays!
But now, neighbor, if you really want to know what's
    fer yer good,
Take yer pop-gun up and travel quicker 'n lightnin
    from this wood!
And if e'er again I catch you sneakin round this
    holler here,
By old Goshen! Betty'll bore you smack and smooth
    through t'other ear!
For this ground is consecrated, and is not for such
    as you;
Now be off, you sneaking puppy, and be careful what
    you do!"
Then he turned to sobbing ESTHER — for excitement's
    quick rebound

Had so left her weak and helpless, she sank weeping
to the ground;

And to shocked and frightened JESSIE, who in silence
had stood by,

Until now there was no danger she cried hard as
she could cry.

Soothing words of kind encouragement so tenderly,
he spake,

Vowing if that rascal harmed them speedy vengeance
he would take,

But all the while maintaining that KING would never
dare,

To execute his threatenings, which were only empty
air!

And fatherly advising her, as he left her at her
door,

Not to tell her husband of it — nor to think about it
more —

"For he cannot mend the matter, and 'twill only give
him pain,

And I know that KING will never dare to try that
thing again!

But if he does, and Betty here is called upon to
sing

Another of her songs to him, then *good bye, Bobby
King!*

But, ESTHER, I must hustle off — or, by the 'tarnal
law,

My wife'll think I've run away with some good
    looking squaw!"
So off into the woods he sprang and soon was lost to
    view,
This strong, athletic, stalwart man, kind-hearted, good,
    and true.

———oo⟡oo———

PART TENTH.

MEDITATIONS OF A VILLAIN—"DO NO MURDER, ROBERT KING!"—MANOMIN'S JOURNEY—THE MIDNIGHT INCENDIARY!

———◦◇◦———

Down in ceaseless, sobbing torrents fell a cold, autumnal rain,
Beating sad and dismal measures on the dripping
  window-pane!
Come and gone had Indian summer, and the naked
  forest trees
Wailed and moaned and tossed their bare arms, cold,
  and shivering in the breeze.
All throughout the leafless forest unobstructed swept
  the eye,
No thick vines or matted branches shut away the
  arching sky.
Leaves of red and brown and purple, white leaves,
  brightly spangled o'er,
Wet and shining gleamed and glistened like a rich
  mosaic floor!

92

ROBERT KING was in his cabin, door and window
    fastened tight,
Grimly brooding o'er his vengeance, by his fitful
    fire light.
In his hand he held a letter — "Yes," he muttered,
    "that's the plan;
Let the sale come off at that time RICHARD is a
    ruined man!
Ah, we'll see, my scornful ESTHER, how you'll writhe,
    and weep and pray!
Oh, I'll make you — as I told you — curse your very
    natal day!
As for that great blustering hunter —— every day
    he passes by
The old wigwam in the hollow, he this very day
    must die!
I'm resolved to stop at nothing, I will teach these
    meddling fools
That 'tis dangerous to be trifling, children like, with
    sharpened tools!"
Then he paused, and every feature wore a dark,
    malignant frown,
Presently he rose, and reaching, took his long bright
    rifle down;
Then again he hesitated, as if fearful, or in doubt,
Suddenly he wrapt an oil-cloth round his rifle and
    set out.

As he neared the lonely wigwam, lo, a figure, tall
and slim,
With a sharp and angry visage, suddenly confronted
him:
"Stay your footsteps, son of evil — leave undone this
wicked thing,
Listen to the God within you — *Do no murder,*
ROBERT KING!"
With averted eyes in terror silently had ROBERT
stood,
Now he raised them, as the voice ceased, — he alone
was in the wood!
Paled his face, short grew his breathings, frightfully
his eyeballs glared —
Then he cursed himself and muttered: "I'm a fool
for being scared!
But I don't quite like this business, "'murder'"
sounds a little rough,
And I reckon, without killing, I can get revenge
enough!"
Like a pluckless beaten spaniel, meanest among
earth's mean men,
He at once retraced his footsteps, slunk again into
his den.

Once again with purest ermine, costly, spotless, soft,
and white,

Winter tenderly enfolded earth's brown bosom from
    the sight.

Every bald old rock or boulder, limb or log beneath
    that sky

Wore a lavish robe of beauty princes were too poor
    to buy.

And the trees that had so sadly cast their garments,
    one by one,

Now, bedecked with winter's diamonds, shone re-
    splendent in the sun!

It was evening, RICHARD THORNTON, holding little
    golden head,

Sat beside his cheerful fire, talking of the summer
    fled,

And of absent, loved MANOMIN, who had gone, a
    week ago,

Far away o'er sheeted prairies, frozen lakes and
    drifts of snow;

Far away through leafless forests, tangled thickets,
    groves of pines,

Far beyond where Crow Wing River with the Red-
    Eye joins and winds,

Far beyond sweet Lake Lelina, where the deep pine
    forests roar,

North of Mix and Ikwe's bosoms, to Lake Hassar's
    pine girt shore.

It was thought a fearful journey for a stalwart man
    to take,

How then more than doubly fearful for a tender girl
    to make?

But "Pewaubeck" and two other lithe limbed warriors
    brought, one day

A short letter from her father, that sick unto death
    he lay

At the trading-post of Hassar, straight her filial
    love arose,

And she bade adieu to comforts, braved at once the
    blinding snows,

Scathing winds, and dismal forests, shrieking in the
    bitter cold,

Giving shelter to rapacious packs of wolves grown
    hunger-bold!

Took no thought of treacherous marshes, miles and
    miles of frozen lakes,

Wind swept prairies, brambled thickets, snow piled
    hollows, drifted brakes;

Urged by that most potent power, strong, deep seated
    filial love, —

Heaven's law of gravitation, binding all its hosts
    above

Down to kindred shining spirits wrapped in earthly
    forms of clay,

Tenderly forever watching, till death rends those
    forms away.

Love, oh love, thou art the power ruling all eternal
    things,

More resistless than the simoon is the flutter of thy
    wings.
Urged, I say, by this resistless power of love she
    faced wild storms,
Boldly braved the King of Terrors in its most ap-
    palling forms.
All that loved and loving circle deeply mourned her
    dreary task,
But that she should hush love's pleadings and remain,
    they could not ask.
So with fur-lined skirt and mantle, swan-down socks
    upon her feet,
Over-drawn by finest doeskin moccasins embroidered
    neat,
A broad girdle trimmed with feathers, leathern pouch
    of brightest red,
And a quilted hood of otter, snugly fitting to her
    head,
Fur-lined mittens and long armlets thoughtful little
    JESSIE'S gift,
Nice light snow-shoes, made by HARRY, to defy the
    deepest drift;
Blessed and kissed and well provisioned, bundled
    snugly, dry and warm,
They committed her, one morning, with wet eyes
    unto the storm!
And as RICHARD thought about it, on that howling
    wintry night,

Sitting there in all the comfort of his cheerful fire
 light,
Fears and doubts and wild misgivings made his
 anxious forehead damp,
And his spirit seemed to seek her in her distant
 snow-bound camp!
Then mature reflection whispered that her guides
 were good and true,
And she would not lack a comfort that their cunning
 wood craft knew.

Esther plied her busy needle with a calm, contented air,
While her dear old father slumbered sweetly in the
 rocking chair.
Lonesome Harry read the papers, heaving now and
 then a sigh,
As among the crowded columns rapidly he glanced
 his eye.
" Father," suddenly he uttered, looking up as if surprised,
" Do you know that in this paper all our lands are
 advertised
To be sold in February? Oh, it is a burning
 shame!
Many a poor man down the valley will be driven
 from his claim;

Many a poor, hard working fellow, toiling on this
    wild frontier,
Nobly struggling with his hardships, laboring on from
    year to year,
Thinking that his dear Columbia, for whose glory he
    would die,
Surely will his hard earned acres kindly give him,
    by and by,
Now will find on his heart's altar his sweet flowers
    of belief
Withered, blighted, turned to ashes and his house-
    hold come to grief!"
"Yes, my son, it is distressing, and I thank the
    God of fate
It is certain honest Lincoln will assume the chair of
    State!
Oh, he knows the people's struggles, and I feel con-
    vinced he will
Recommend and give his sanction to a liberal Home-
    stead Bill!
We are safe, if nothing happens, BURBANK offers for
    my grain
More than would suffice to purchase our claim o'er
    and o'er again!
DARLING tells me that the threshers, though obstruct-
    ed by the snow
At Osakis, will most surely come on in a day or so.

Let us therefore be preparing, and to BARR and
    BEDMAN speak,
And to CANFIELD and PREFOUNTAIN, for assistance
    by next week,
And if then our oats shall yield us half the bushels
    all expect,
At the sale we may be able some poor neighbor
    to protect.
JESSIE, go and get the Bible, HARRY, son, draw
    up your chair;
Let us thank our Heavenly Father for his ever
    constant care."

In the small and silent hours of that same cold,
    winter night
Stole a form across the timber in the glaring, white
    moonlight.
On, to RICHARD's log-built stables stealthily it made
    its way,
Stables straw-roofed and begirt by stacks of oats and
    ricks of hay.
Suddenly, above the oat-stacks, leaped a wild and
    lurid flame!
Oh, a deed so mean and dastard should have crim-
    soned hell with shame!
In those stables RICHARD's cattle — firmly fastened
    by the head,

Burned and bellowed, roared and roasted till their
    tortured spirits fled.
Wakened by the awful roaring of the flames and
    bellowing stock,
Forth he rushed! Oh, God, how dreadful, wild and
    stunning was the shock!
Souls of tears and hearts of pity, realize, oh, if
    you can,
Deep within your inmost feelings, all the ruin of
    this man!
Ruin of this hopeful spirit, who, but now, with bended
    head,
Had poured out its love to Heaven, and gone trust-
    ingly to bed!
Faith persistent under evil is that virtue's highest
    grade ;
Faith to know the hand that blesses wields for good
    the lightning's blade ;
Faith like this was RICHARD THORNTON'S — in mis-
    fortune's darkest day,
Steady, brilliant, undiminished, shone its white celes-
    tial ray.
When the first wild shock was over, though it swept
    him bald and bare,
He convened his little circle, on his altar laid a
    prayer !
And although completest ruin stared him grimly in
    the face,

No upbraidings marred his offering to the holy Throne
of Grace.

He reminded not the Father worse than other men
he fared,

But he prayed for greater patience, thanked Him that
their lives were spared!

Prayed that in the hidden future his poor efforts
might be blessed.

Then with quiet resignation once again he sought
his rest.

PART ELEVENTH.

SAD REFLECTIONS — PAT DEEGAN'S LETTER — THE SALE —
TRIUMPH OF KING — MANOMIN ARRIVES — "DICK
THORNTON IS ALL RIGHT!" — SUMMARY PRO-
CEEDINGS — "BITING BETTY"
SINGS AGAIN!!

————◆————

SAD and tearful were the faces gathered round
    that morning meal,
Though with sweet contrition humble, stricken, yet,
    they could but feel.
God of heaven, who would help them? Their kind
    neighbors were poor, too;
Who would lighten their affliction? What, oh, what
    were they to do?
"Write to friends," suggested HARRY, friends who
    live in Syracuse."
"Yes, we will, but I am fearful it will prove of
    little use.

103

Business men are cold and cautious, and unless they
    see your need,
Calls for help, howe'er pathetic, they will seldom
    ever heed !
Still, it is our solemn duty every honest way to try
To retrieve an adverse fortune, passing not the un-
    likeliest by."
On the Cinder Road was living PATRICK DEEGAN,
    and his name,
If it did not tell his story, told at once from whence
    he came.
In the mist of years departed, like a rainbow, stood
    a day
RICHARD THORNTON had advanced him means to buy
    a horse and dray.
Oft to him had HARRY written, of their wild but
    glorious fare,
And of lovely Minnesota's splendid lakes and bracing
    air,
Of her prairies, starred with flowers, of her forests
    full of deer,
Of her sweet cascades and rivers, and her fountains,
    pure and clear;
Unto him, the touching story of their fortunes, so
    adverse,
In a letter, now did HARRY with simplicity re-
    hearse;

But he did not ask for money, never dreamed that
    source to try,
Not believing PATRICK DEEGAN ever laid a dollar
    by.
But as hearts, o'ercharged with sorrow, seeking chan-
    nels of relief,
In some sympathetic bosom pour a portion of their
    grief,
In that sense and spirit only, without thought of help
    the while,
Wrote he to that generous scion of the little Emerald
    Isle.
Graphic letters RICHARD also wrote to many an
    eastern friend,
But their answers brought no money his bad prospects
    to amend.
Meanwhile on Time's rapid current came the dreaded
    day at hand,
That should dawn upon them homeless, strip them of
    the cherished land
Where they had, with faithful labor, built and plowed,
    · and fenced and sown,
In their trustful hearts believing it must ever be
    their own !
When, at last, that wretched morning lengthened into
    turbid day,
Lo, there came this glorious letter, which had long
    been on its way:

"Arrah, HARRY, me darlint, yer swate little letther
　Came nately to hand on this cowld blissid day;—
I was thrashin' me hans, an a cussin the weather,
　An pitying poor Hock, in the shafts of his dray,
When up stips the postman, ould DINNIS McFRAZES,
　Wid the breath on his whiskers like foam on the seas,
An' his frost-bitten nose all as rid as blue blazes
　Wid a "'Here, Mister DEEGAN,'s a letther for yees!'"
'Twas too cowld for a job, an was fast gettin cowlder,
　So I whistles to Hock, an I jumps on the dray,
"'Och, sure, ye'll not mind, when ye're fifty years owlder,'"
　Says I to me conscience, "the loss of this day.'"
So, HARRY, mavourneen, yer folks are in throuble!
　Ye're burned out, ye think, by that rascally KING,
May the divil, bad cess to'im, bend him up double,
　An in hell's hottest corner his owld carcass fling!
An it's all for the lack of a wee bit of sphilter,
　Some two hundred dollars, I'm thinkin ye said,
Ye'd be swept clane and dry, as a tin year owld philter,
　Wid never a shingle to cover yer head;—
Och, HARRY, ye sphalpeen, was ye thinkin PAT DEEGAN,
　Wid a long woman's stocking-leg chock full of gould,
Could slape in his bid, like owld miserly REEGAN,
　While the frinds of his harte were turned out in the cowld?
Not a word now, ye gossoon, I've put up the money,
　Jist double ye nades, in a nate little bag,
And up to St. Cloud, by express, to yees, honey,
　It will come jist as fast as the buljine can wag!
An I wish, be me sowl, I could come wid it, HARRY,
　To make sure, me boy, that it didn't come late,
But I can't, an so hoping it will not miscarry,
　　　　　I am, Yours,
　　　　　　　　　　　PATRICK DEEGAN.
　　　Plase acknowledge resate.

Softly down they laid the letter, while a spirit of
    relief
Sunned away the gloomy shadow of their heavy-
    hearted grief.
Though this money had not reached them, could not
    for a fortnight more,
Yet they knew that safely waiting at St. Cloud in
    BURBANK'S store,
It was subject to their order — forty eagles, all in
    gold!
Ha! the thought was vivifying — made the drooping
    spirit bold!
Sure, this tangible assurance, must induce the auc-
    tioneer
To forego the sale of their claim till their money
    reached them here :
" Yes," he said, "if none demand it, thereon hinges
    everything ! "
Sank the mercury of their spirits at the icy thought
    of KING!
Ah, their fears were but too real, all their efforts
    proved in vain,
KING exulted o'er them homeless, he had triumphed
    once again!
And he sent them instant warning that before an-
    other day
He would come and take possession, they must move
    at once away.

Sturdy squatters, grim and scowling, gathered round
    in little bands,
Capped with fur and clothed in buckskin, carrying
    rifles in their hands!
They were taking anxious council what had best be
    done with KING:
Should they hang him, whip him, shoot him, had they
    best do anything?
"Well, now, boys," said Uncle DARLING, "I've a
    feeling that to-night
Something is ago'n' to happen that will bring this
    thing out right!"
At that moment, at the town-house, rose a wild and
    ringing shout,
Then another, and another — what were all those
    cheers about?
Once again they were repeated, hats flew up into
    the air,
What the deuce could be the meaning of such wild
    excitement there?
Through the gate-way rushed a neighbor screaming
    to them with delight:
"MANOMIN's come with loads of money! hurrah!
    DICK THORNTON is all right!"
ROBERT KING was quickly summoned, 'twas a call
    he did not dare
Disobey, and soon the villain came into their presence
    there.

"Robert King," said Uncle Darling, "we have
sent for you to come

Here to give up Thornton's patent, pledging you
three times the sum

That it cost you, will you do it?"—"No, sir, never
while I live;

'Twas my right to buy his claim, sir, and no man shall
make me give

Cringingly a right my country's sacred laws vouch-
safe to me;

Money cannot buy that claim, sir, all your plans are
vain, you see."

Jo. James then informed the circle that Manomin
wished to say

A word or two upon this matter, ere they let King
go away.

Stepping lightly from the circle to the centre forth
she stood,

Queenly in her radiant beauty, little empress of the
wood!

"Friends and neighbors! a plain story I will tell,
brief as I can,

Of the savage misdemeanors and the *crimes* of this
bad man:

Years ago, when Esther Thornton was a sweet,
unwedded maid,

Presumptuous seige to her affections this persistent
villain laid,

And most stormily insisted she should yield and be
    his wife,   .

Threatening her, if she refused him, with his hatred
    all her life.

But she scorned his threats as every brave, true-
    hearted woman would,

And she married RICHARD THORNTON, first among
    the pure and good.

After many years of scheming, ventured plots and
    sore defeats,

Hellish industry succeeded and he turned them in
    the streets!

Seeking no retaliation for his utter overthrow,

RICHARD THORNTON left the precincts of his mean,
    inveterate foe —

Foe without a shade of reason, who, to further wreak
    his hate,

Like a wolf has tracked his victim to this distant
    frontier state.

In the woods he meets with ESTHER and insults her,
    but his ear

Tells the story of reprisals made by Uncle DARLING
    here!

All last summer, RICHARD THORNTON, most persist-
    ent, soon and late,

Toiled among the sheaves and winrows, sums of
    money to create

For the high and noble purpose of maintaining well
in hand

Funds, perchance, to help a neighbor, while securing
his own land.

One month since I left his dwelling, passed his oat-
stacks one by one,

Saw with joy their golden shoulders bare and glistening in the sun!

And his stable full of cattle and his great brown
ricks of hay;

How these proofs of his abundance cheered me on
my weary way!

Three weeks since, while all were sleeping, stealthily
a villain came,

And he wrapt that wealth collective in one great,
consuming flame:

And an Indian says, who saw him, that this man,
this fiend, this thing,

Who so causeless spoiled a neighbor was this villain,
ROBERT KING!"

What a fierce wild shout of anger round that listening
circle ran,

And a dozen gleaming rifles straight were leveled
at the man!

But MANOMIN into order quickly waved them with
her hand,

Magic-like she quelled the feelings of that roused,
excited band.

At her sign a sprightly Indian promptly stepped into
    the ring —

" Neighbors, this is BUNGEE-WAUPOSE, he it was
    who witnessed KING

Do that dreadful deed of arson, for which crime men
    often die " —

" 'Tis a lie ! " screamed KING in terror, " 'tis a weak
    and wicked lie ! "

DARLING stopped him and MANOMIN quietly began
    again :

BUNGEE-WAUPOSE speaks no English, thinking that
    he should not gain

Any credit by attempting what he could not render
    clear,

He at once set out to meet me, and we made forced
    marches here !

I arrived, and quickly learning RICHARD's claim to
    KING was sold,

Sent and offered thrice the purchase to that bad man
    there, in gold.

But you heard him scorn the offer, heard him vaunt-
    ing of his right !

Oh, his right to burn the substance of a neighbor
    in the night !

He has forced poor RICHARD THORNTON twice to
    drain grief's bitter cup,

Now, my neighbors, all I ask is, make him give
    that patent up ! "

Scarcely had she ceased, ere DARLING, reaching forth
    his brawny hand,
Roughly seized KING by the collar — "Now, then,
    villian, we *demand,*
Without slightest compensation, that you give to
    THORNTON, here,
What is his, or else, by Heaven! we will make it
    cost you dear!"
"Do your worst, I do not fear you!" — "All right,
    Mister BOBBY KING!
Bring a rope, BARR, quicker 'n lightnin', and we'll
    see about this thing!"
The rope was brought and noosed about him, o'er a
    beam one end was flung,
By the neck, before he knew it, high the struggling
    victim hung.
In a moment more they dropped him, dizzy, strangled,
    and half blind;
Ah, this summary proceeding quickly changed the
    rascal's mind;
For his ear had caught the order: "Up again, boys,
    pull away!"
"Men!" he cried, "hold on for God's sake! I will
    do whate'er you say!"
"All right, boys, bring out a table, and a pen and
    inkstand, too;
Now, sir, sign this patent over, that is all we want
    of you."

Down he sat while angry tremors, like an ague, shook
    his frame,

And he formed a hellish purpose as he calmly wrote
    his name.

"ROBERT KING, said Uncle DARLING, as he rose
    to go away,

"Stop a moment, for this council has another word
    to say:

In two days you are required Douglas County, sir,
    to leave;

If the third day finds you lingering, punishment you
    will receive;

On the fourth day, any person, red or white, about
    this town

Is commissioned, if he meets you, like a dog to shoot
    you down!"

KING passed out all grim and silent, not a word had
    he to say —

Then across the lake to JAMES' nearly all adjourned
    straightway,

There to have a wild reunion, songs and dancing,
    fun and beer

Over RICHARD's change of fortune, just as ruin seem-
    ed so near.

But MANOMIN and the THORNTONS at the town-house
    stayed behind

To partake a bounteous supper, and with brimming,
    joyful mind

They drew up around the table, and discussed what
    seemed to be
A most strange and providential foiling of their
    enemy.

Uncle DARLING started homeward through the woods
    a nearer way —
"Ah, what's that?" A long dark object, stretched
    behind a log-heap, lay!
Boldly outlined on the white snow 'neath a full
    moon's golden glare,
"'Tis a man! 'tis KING, by Heaven! what's the
    rascal doing there?"
DARLING crouched behind a tree-root, bared by tem-
    pest in its wrath,
By and by there came the THORNTONS and MANO-
    MIN down the path.
See! KING moves, his leveled rifle bears on RICH-
    ARD THORNTON'S brain!
A flash, a crash! ah, lifeless villain, *"Biting Betty"*
    sang again!

PART TWELFTH.

———◆◇◆———

ROUND the hearth of RICHARD THORNTON sunny
    hearts rejoiced once more;
In the grave of KING was buried all their appre-
    hensions, sore,
And about their cheerful fire they have gathered
    now, to hear
All that happened to MANOMIN in those thirty days
    of fear.
But her story was a brief one: She had found her
    father dead
When she reached the termination of her journeying,
    she said;
All his furs and goods to BOLIEAUX by her order
    then, were sold,
Many thousand dollars bringing, which was paid to
    her in gold.

" Then, with sense of trouble weighing sad and heavy
    on my heart —
Trouble to my living dear ones — with my money
    I did start;
And one morning BUNGEE-WAUPOSE met and told
    me of the deed
That had robbed you of your substance — how I
    urged my guides to speed!
Every day I fought the snow-drifts, and at night
    would sit and cry
At the slowness of my progress! How I longed
    for wings to fly!
And with joy and apprehension how my throbbing
    heart did swell
When I saw the town-house chimneys! This is all
    I have to tell.
Now, my darling foster-father — best among all men
    I 've known —
Use this money I have brought you, freely, as it
    were your own.
Send to generous PATRICK DEEGAN twice the sum
    he loaned to you,
As a meet reward for friendship, which is rarely
    found so true.
Not a word, now, father THORNTON, for I owe you
    this, and more — "
Here a heavy rapping sounded loudly on the outer
    door.

HARRY rose and swung it open; on its threshold
    calmly stood

That strange presence of the Hollow, silent GAFFER
    of the wood!

"Peace to all within this dwelling!" in a kindly
    tone he said,

"Lo, I bear a message to you from the régions of
    the dead!

Dead to every low desire, dead to all that is not
    right,

But alive to love and brotherhood, to wisdom and
    to light!

Let us sit around this table, and a moment join our
    hands,

There are hosts of spirits hovering from the inner,
    brighter lands!"

All drew up around the table but in RICHARD
    THORNTON's eyes

Shone a look of incredulity and wondering surprise.

He had never been to GAFFER's nor had ever given
    ear

To the mystifying stories told about him far and
    near,

Until HARRY's strange experience taught him pos-
    sibly there might

Be laws in God's economy he did not know aright.

Scarcely had they formed the circle ere some sturdy
    raps were heard,

Then a strain of forest music, like the warbling of
    a bird;

Then the table mounted upward, as if from the floor
    repelled,

Next the name of MARY WARREN by the alphabet
    was spelled!

"Oh my God!" said ESTHER'S father, pale and
    trembling, "can it be

MARY WARREN — my own MARY — is within this
    room with me?"

" Yes, oh yes, ERASTUS WARREN, I am MARY, your
    own wife!"

Said a soft voice close behind him — "and though in
    the inner life,

I am with you every moment, for the day is near
    at hand

When you, too, my dear companion, will be added
    to our band.

Do not think the spirit's heaven is away in realms
    afar,

In a walled up golden city, or in some bright distant
    star.

Heaven is Love, and Love is God, and God is here
    and everywhere,

Hence 'tis natural that our heaven should be where
    our dear ones are!

With what longing I have waited for this blessed
    hour to come,

Ere you crossed the dreaded valley, to inform you
of your home ;
Of your home of love eternal, home of wisdom and
of light,
Where, your earthly errors spurning, you will read
God's laws aright!
You will learn that every evil is the body's attribute ;
With the body that it perishes as perishes the brute!
And the qualities immortal, such as fellowship and
love,
Are the only things the spirit takes along with it
above !
Oh, we have no use for envy, have no need of hate
or pride,
Lying, jealousy, or selfishness, or evil, else, beside,
And having then no need of them, oh, does it not
seem plain —
As God ne'er made a useless thing, or gave a useless
pain —
They should fall with falling matter — being of and
for the earth,
Not arising with the spirit to its brighter, higher
birth.
See the caterpillar creeping on its belly in the dirt,
Feeding on decaying matter, — by repulsiveness be-
girt;
Mark the butterfly — its spirit — how it mounts on
wings away,

Nestling down within the flowers, sipping honey all
    the day;
Shut your eyes against this lesson, oh obdurate heart-
    ed men,
Let your Chinese wall of prejudice keep truth with-
    out, and then
Learn too late, if truth and wisdom in the body be
    not sought,
If the "golden rule" and charity on earth be not out-
    wrought,
As a penalty, your spirits will be naked, weak, and
    poor,
When your guardians kindly bear you to this love-lit
    angel shore;
And each one in ways of loveliness be long a puny
    thing,
Wanting years to reach its God-head. Thus it is
    with ROBERT KING,
Who is here, too weak to manifest — and wishes me
    to say
That through ignorance and prejudice his life was
    thrown away;
And the high and noble lessons in his sinfulness he
    spurned,
Under many disadvantages now slowly must be learn-
    ed;
That his dark and stormy passions did not know this
    second birth—

They are buried with his body in the bosom of the
    earth —

Yet their mem'ries blot his spirit like a moth-patch
    or a stain,

So he comes to ask forgiveness, for the many hours
    of pain

He has caused you, RICHARD, ESTHER, and each one
    within this room, —

Oh, he sees he is forgiven, swiftly vanishes his
    gloom!

Brighter glows the God within him, wild with joy his
    pulses dance!

O'er the bright celestial highway swiftly now will
    he advance!

By and by, returning earthward, you will find him
    strong and bright,

Purged of all self-condemnation, hallowed by Eternal
    Right!

He will often stand beside you — though so distant
    seems this shore —

And will give you love and guidance where he gave
    you hate before!

As the clock ticks off the seconds, so remorseless, one
    by one,

You will all come dropping homeward when your
    primal life is done.

You will then behold how different is the great
    creative plan

From the narrow, cramped conceptions of materialistic
man.
You will learn that every erring soul on sin's wild
ocean tossed
Safe in God's conservatory moors at last where naught
is lost!
You will learn that the aspirings of the selfish sons
of earth,
Pride of wealth, and place, and title, and aristocratic
birth,
Are mere wallowings in the mire — all unworthy the
great prize
That awaits you in God's mansions, in the bosom of
the skies!
There, at last, I'm sure to greet you, on those ever
verdant lawns!
So, good night, have faith and patience, till your day
of promise dawns!"

Quickly passed the broken winter to that happy household, there,
All their joys were pure and perfect, not a harsh
word or a care
Ever ribbed with gloomy wrinkles the calm forehead
of their peace!
Indeed, their sum of happiness seemed daily to increase.

But at last that charm was broken by a shock that
    shook the world!

A tempest flight of treason's shells from rebel cannon
    hurled!

And Columbia's cry for armies, from old Sumpter's
    battered wall,

And the thundering tread of millions answering to
    that clarion call!

On the flashing wings of lightning, through the art-
    eries of the mail,

To the nation's farthest corners flew the wild, ex-
    citing tale!

From the workshop and the furrow, from the ware-
    house and the strand,

From the cities and the forests men were hurrying,
    gun in hand;

From Oregon's wild mountains, and from California's
    mines

Hosts of large-lunged, brawny patriots came to swell
    the loyal lines!

All the land was hung with banners! from tall masts
    and taller spires,

From roofs and windows, cliffs and poles, forth flamed
    those altar fires!

Ah, this national uprising was a spectacle so vast,

All wonder-struck and motionless the world looked
    on aghast!

The poor slave's millennial morning dawned at length
    upon his sight!
Struck forever from his horizon was slavery's wretch-
    ed night!
Gross forms and base conditions went staggering to
    their fall,
And an era, bright and shining, full of blessings unto
    all,
By High Heaven's Great Sanhedrim was decreed
    the very day
Rebel cannon rang the curtain up on treason's tragic
    play!
To the listening circle HARRY read the news that
    April night,
And a sense of sure bereavement made their hearts
    grow still and white.
For they saw a noble purpose shining forth in every
    line
And lineament of that brave boy's heroic face di-
    vine!
One bugle-blast had snatched him up, crowned with
    iron his fair brow,
Built a wall of steel between them, he was all his
    country's now!
But they murmured not at laying even him, their
    only boy,
Their bright glory of the present, their perspective's
    calmer joy,

On the altar of their country, trusting Him, whose
    care profound,

Noteth even every little bird that falleth to the
    ground !

Still, a painful silence settled on those hearts, but
    now so bright;

One by one they bade each other then a kind yet
    sad good night !

Poor MANOMIN sought her little room, and shutting
    to the door,

In one swift wild rush of agony sank sobbing to the
    floor !

Alas, poor lonely wild wood flower, her heart, that
    had so late

Been rendered by the touch of death so void and
    desolate,

Had warmed again beneath the sun of HARRY's
    genial eyes ;

And, oh, he filled and spanned that heart as rainbows
    do the skies !

Alas, poor lone MANOMIN, she knew no youth like
    him

Could for a moment sit at ease when treason, armed
    and grim,

Sat at the door-ways of our land, with insults, taunts
    and sneers,

And robbed and burned steamboats and trains, like
    filthy buccaneers !

She felt within her inmost soul that he, with purpose
    strongly set,
Would rest not till in loyal lines the sun gleamed on
    his bayonet!
"And, oh, how many must be killed! Great God
    above me, must I feel
This flower goeth from my heart to be cut down by
    Southern steel?
Oh, those lists of killed and wounded! how we all
    shall dread to read!
Lest hearts we *now* think desolate, *shall be desolate
    indeed!*"
Morning dawned, and every riser, as they came into
    the room,
Saw a little sight that saddened, deeper still, their
    spirit's gloom:
It was only HARRY'S rifle standing up beside the door,
And a little bundle lying at its breech upon the floor!

PART THIRTEENTH.

---◆◆◆---

'TWAS an early July morning, fresh and cool the
dew-drops hung,
Bending down the heavy meadow-grass, where scythe-
stones gaily rung,
And sturdy brown armed mowers laid the wild thick
harvest low,
With such ease and grace of motion that it seemed
but play to mow!
With an even stroke the mowers swung their scythes
at easy pace,
Till at length some boastful whetstone rang a chal-
lenge for a race!
With firm lip and swelling muscles grandly swayed
each lithe form then,
And the merest boys among them stoutly played the
part of men.

128

Uncle DARLING, from the centre — with wide swarth
and forward tread —
One by one cut round the mowers, till he came far
out ahead;
And, with rollicking good nature, wiped the sweat
from off his face,
Slily asking if the "chap was lost that started that
'ar race?"
ESTHER's father bore the luncheon and the water to
the field;
But his sinews were not strong enough the manly
scythe to wield;
Though on this very morning long and well the rake
he plied,
Till wearied out, he tottered home, his strength most
sorely tried.
He bathed his face, and JESSIE, dusting off his easy
chair,
Clambering fondly up beside him, gently combed his
silvery hair.
"Oh, grandpa, don't you wonder now, where HARRY
is to-day?
Has he really gone to kill some one, or is it only
play?
And do you think they'd kill him, too? Oh, that
would be so sad —
Why is it, grandpa, that some folks will always be
so bad?

It seems to me, if I was God, I don't believe I
would

Let folks be born, unless I knew they surely would
be good!"

Then moistening her finger-tips upon her little tongue,

She curled his pliant locks and said, "Now, grandpa,
you look young!

I wonder if you'll have white hair away up in the
sky?

Wait, wait! hold still! I think I see a winker in
your eye!"

With corner of her pinafore, twirled round, with tender care,

She wiped away, with gentle touch, the irritating
hair.

Then laid her little damask cheek against his wrinkled
face,

And round his neck entwined her arms in silent, fond
embrace.

Strong voices roused her, she looked up, "See, grandpa, only see! —

Here come the men! 'tis not yet noon! What can
the matter be?"

MANOMIN, who had seen them too, came forth with
blanching cheek —

"Oh, have you heard bad news from *him?* — speak,
father THORNTON, speak!"

"No, no, my child, we've only heard a battle has
    been fought,
In which our army did not do the valiant deeds it
    ought.
That after they had fairly won the honors of the
    day,
They suddenly, in panic, fled, flinging their arms
    away!
The Minnesota boys were there — but here, I think,
    you'll find
A letter from the lad whose fate just now disturbed
    your mind.
And here is one for mother, too — now all draw round
    about.
We'll hear what HARRY has to say about this shame-
    ful rout."
MANOMIN had her letter clutched and, waiting for
    no more,
Gone fairly flying to her room, and promptly locked
    the door.
We'll leave her with her beating heart, and face
    blanched white as snow,
And hear the letter RICHARD, now, is reading down
    below: —
"I am writing to you, mother, on this sultry July
    night,
To assure you of my safety, and to tell you of the
    fight:

For the horrors of that struggle who more vividly
    can tell

Than one who faced that storm of lead and hurricane
    of shell?

'Twas a glorious, silv'ry Sunday and the morning's
    spicy breath

Gave no warning to the many soon to be baptized
    in death!

For sweet peace herself, seemed dwelling in the
    silent foliage green,

And from each shining blade of grass to be smiling
    so serene,

That it really did not seem, mother, amid so *much*
    of life,

We should all so soon be facing old grim Death in
    mortal strife!

As we wound along the valleys, over spreading fields,
    and farms,

How the lovely landscape twinkled with the glitter
    of our arms!

Filing up the sloping hill-sides, threading some long,
    deep ravine,

With our bayonets all gleaming, — — 'twas indeed a
    splendid scene!

Oh, there seemed to be such power in our firm'
    united tread —

In our hands a freeman's weapon, and a just God
    overhead —

That it did not make me wonder when was heard
    the opening gun
To hear our brave boys' answering cheers! The
    battle had begun!
Oh, my mother, had you seen us as we moved across
    the field!
Vainly, proudly, fondly dreaming that the foe would
    quickly yield,
You, too, would have caught the quickening that in-
    spired MEAGHER'S braves
When they flung away their garments, and went rush-
    ing to their graves!
Brave, iron-hearted HEINTZLEMAN soon swept along,
    where rose
Thick wreaths of smoke above the trees that hid
    our wary foes;
Gallant BURNSIDE'S men responded with a wild and
    ringing shout,
As their glittering line of battle they flung quickly,
    fiercely out!
And uniting with brave PORTER and the generous,
    loyal SPRAGUE,
Swept the rebels to destruction, like the besom of
    a plague!
Then swiftly, through that fire and flame, way out
    upon the right,
By MILLER led, *our* gallant boys went cheering to
    the fight!

I can scarcely tell you, mother, as the first, fierce
    storm of lead
Came whistling through our solid ranks, or hurtling
    overhead,
Of my spirit's wild sensations, or the throbs my
    pulses made,
And though it seemed like fear, mother, yet I did not
    feel afraid!
It is true, my heart a moment, just a moment, ceased
    to beat,
As we bent before the opening storm of furious leaden
    sleet;
It is true I dodged a little, and a moment held my
    breath
As the bullets whizzed above me, but it was not fear
    of death;
'Twas the instinct that God gives us to avoid the
    fatal stroke —
But I lost it, in a moment, 'mid the battle's flame
    and smoke,
And my heart at once responded to our gallant leader's
    call:
"' Be steady, boys! close up the ranks whene'er your
    comrades fall!'"
Just then the Black Horse Cavalry charged fiercely
    on our flank —
But, ah! the bloody wine of death full many a rider
    drank!

They paused and turned, then fled, and formed, and
  once again they came,
But all in vain, they could *not live* before our deadly
  aim!
And hotter, fiercer than before, the wild fight raged
  around, —
Identity, itself, seemed lost amid the dreadful sound!
But we fought on bravely, mother, till arose the
  cheering cry:
"'Hurrah, hurrah, brave, loyal hearts! the beaten
  rebels fly!'"
Then with cheers all forward springing how we made
  those woods resound!
And, like sheep, the frightened rebels went flying
  o'er the ground!
But there came a check, a halting, and we *heard a
  distant drum!*
Saw clouds of dust, a cry arose that JOHNSTON'S *men
  had come!!*
At first there came an anxious pause, then confidence
  seemed lost —
Then *panic,* wild, resistless spread among our loyal
  host!
The brave and dauntless HEINTZLEMAN rode back
  and forth in vain!
Those terror-stricken, broken lines could not be formed
  again!

It was a painful sight to see those men, who, true
    and good,
The whole fierce shock of rebel arms so lately had
    withstood,
Now turn their backs upon their foes, abandon every
    gun,
Throw down their arms and leave the field upon an
    abject run!
But naught could stem that shameful tide, resistless
    it rolled on,
And swept across Potomac's bridge and into Wash-
    ington!
The gallant dead and wounded ones were left just
    where they fell;
Oh, would to God I did not have this shameful truth
    to tell!
I grieved enough while marching back at close of
    that sad day,
To see, all round, the signs of flight, the *debris* of
    the fray!
Spectators' hacks and tumbrils lay all shivered on
    the ground!
And guns and pistols, hats and coats, were thickly
    strewn around!
But all of these might well be spared, aye more than
    treble these,
To purchase one poor, wounded man a single hour
    of ease.

Or have placed our dead with honor, in a grave
their valor won,
With their starry flag above them, bravely waving
in the sun!
But their battles are all over, they have laid their
muskets down,
And across the shining river each has taken up a
crown!
They are gathered with God's children, in the pearly
courts above,
Weaving garlands of nepenthe in the starry looms
of love!
They are treading paths of glory in the endless sea
of spheres,
Where no earthly computations can denominate the
years!
Our neighborhood has lost but one — BILL ARM-
STRONG, "Stuttering Bill,"
Whose death, I know, with sad regrets, each neigh-
bor's heart will fill.
'Twas just before the rout, and he was fighting by
my side,
A grape-shot struck him, and he sank, without a
groan, and died.
Brave "Stuttering Bill," no truer heart e'er rushed
into the fray!
No purer patriot gave his life for Freedom on that
day!

Who, think you, that I saw among brave MEAGHER'S
    headlong boys —

Whose ringing cheers arose above the battle's deafen-
    ing noise?

Why, PATRICK DEEGAN, to be sure — God's blessing
    on his head —

You should have seen him charging through those
    fearful storms of lead!

He recognized me on the field, though swiftly rush-
    ing by,

And called out, "'HARRY, are ye there? God kape
    yees, me brave b'y!'"

GAFFER asks to be remembered. Let me say for
    him, just here,

He is bravery incarnate, knows no sentiment of fear;

Watches o'er me like a father, shares my tent, my
    couch and mess,

And my slightest hint of illness seems to put him
    in distress.

Love to all the dear ones, mother; tell MANOMIN
    I shall write

To her, too, before retiring. Bless you, mother, and
    good night!"

PART FOURTEENTH.

---◆◇◆---

OH, parents, you whose sons have gone forth from
your hearthstone's light,
Clothed with your love and prayers and tears, to
battle for the right,
Who can appreciate like you the hopes, the fears,
the joys,
That are awakened in your breasts by letters from
your boys?
Oh, maidens, with your loves in camps, you whom
battles fill with gloom,
Weep and laugh with poor MANOMIN in the quiet
of her room.
How she fed upon that letter! How, beneath its
magic power
Did her heart burst into blossom, as the sun unfolds
a flower!

159

She read it and re-read it o'er, kissed it, and again
    she read,
Bore it in her bosom all the day, at night, beneath
    her head,
Would lay upon it and would dream of hearing rifles
    roar,
And wake and tremble with a fear of seing *him* no
    more!

The war waged on and armies grew and blows fell
    thick on every hand,
By sea, by shore, in swamp, and glade, the shock of
    battles shook the land.
The bloody day at Wilson's Creek, where brave, true-
    hearted LYON fell,
And that fierce fight at Lexington, where MULLIGAN
    behaved so well,
The crimson mem'ries of Ball's Bluff, where sainted
    BAKER calmly died,
And the red record of Belmont, where rebel numbers
    were defied,
The fierce, wild fight in Beaufort Bay, where old
    New England's valiant sons
To South Car'lina's recreant knaves taught loyalty
    with Dahlgren guns;
The Drainsville triumphs, and the fights at Middle
    and at Silver Creek.

Where GARFIELD won and TORRENCE made the fright-
    ened rebels cover seek;
Mill Spring, where Minnesota boys piled up the
    traitors on the snow,
Where Ninth Ohio bravely fought and FRY laid
    ZOLLIKOFFER low,
Fort Henry and Fort Donelson, where western valor
    brightly shone,
And Roanoke, with all its forts, and North Car'lina's
    coast our own,
The struggle with the "Merrimac," that made all
    Europe's navies reel
And shriek to see the age of wood go down before
    the age of steel;
Pea Ridge, where SIGEL saved the day and BEN.
    McCULLOUGH justly bled,
And Newbern's sanguinary fight, where noble BURN-
    SIDE bravely led;
And SHIELDS' wild strife at Winchester, where bright-
    ly shone Ohio men,
And POPE's bold engineering scheme, that gave us
    Island Number Ten,
And Pittsburg Landing's bloody fray, and New Or-
    leans' great naval fight,
That filled all Europe with dismay, and all our
    country with delight;
And Fort Pulaski's ragged rents, fierce work to be so
    quickly done,

That showed the world how forts will melt before a
    single Parrott gun —
All these wi d doings filled the land, and kept excite-
    ment's life alive,
Yet, discontented murmurs rose, like buzzings from
    an angry hive.
Some blamed some praised, all grumbled loud and
    all some little fault would find —
Oh, may God bless the patriot man, that battles with
    contented mind !
Full many a letter HARRY wrote while prone in
    idleness he lay
In front of Yorktown, but at last the word was:
    " Strike the tents to-day ! "
Keen LEE had drawn his forces off as silent as an
    evening wind
And left McCLELLAN, cautiously, to feel his way
    along behind !
But " Little MACK " had glorious stuff in that great,
    splendid army there —
Impetuous men, but brave withal, and quick to do,
    and bold to dare,
Who would not let the rebels' heels grow cool, when
    fairly on the track,
Although McCLELLAN might be left, they did not care
    what distance back !
And presently the country rang with a great victory's
    trumpet sound —

"Hurrah! hurrah, for Williamsburg!" the million
    echoes flung around.
Again, in RICHARD THORNTON'S circle, anxious dread
    and palsying fear
Made them all averse to hearing, yet most wretched
    not to hear.
Minnesota's loss was fearful, every one they met
    had said —
What if then their darling HARRY, what, oh what, if
    he were dead?
But one morning came a neighbor, and, amid a burst
    of tears,
They perused this noble letter, which at once relieved
    their fears: —

"With the drums of victory sounding and the woods
    with shouts resounding,
Mingled with the mournful patter of the black and
    dismal rain,
I am sitting here, all weary, in this stormy midnight
    dreary,
Writing home to you, dear mother, and MANOMIN,
    once again.
Oh, my brain is wild with battle; still my senses
    seem to rattle
With the volleys of the rifles, and the tumult of the
    fray,

And the cannons' awful thunder, rending heaven and
    earth asunder,
Pouring out their deadly missiles, swiftly sweeping
    life away!
Peace! be still, my ruffled being, calm, my inward
    sense of seeing,
While I tell two souls expectant of the glories we
    have won;
And our brave boys' deeds of valor, and the ghastly
    looks of pallor
On the rebel chieftains' faces when the chivalry all
    run!
Oh, we whipped the rascals roundly, beat them fairly,
    thrashed them soundly,
As their list of killed and wounded, and their missing
    ones will tell,
As will our brave heroes lying stabbed and mangled,
    dead and dying,
Along the line where HOOKER for eight hours fought
    so well;
And where BERRY'S Michiganders, like a swarm of
    salamanders,
Rushing through the line of fire, fell like lightning
    on the foe,
And where resistless BIRNEY and the lion-hearted
    KEARNEY
Swept a swarm of ragged rebels to the gloomy gulf
    below!

How will shine the future's story with the burning
    deeds of glory

Of Colonel DWIGHT's "Excelsior," and old Massa-
    chusetts' sons

Under BLAISDELL, wildly storming, through the forest
    fiercely swarming,

Singing dirges to those rebels with the voices of their
    guns!

And the brave men PECK was leading — Death's wild
    summons never heeding,

All the day, by fiercely fighting, held a crimsoned
    grove of pines,

Until HANCOCK's heroes, turning, with set teeth and
    eye-balls burning,

Burst with steel and flame and bullet on the yelling
    rebel lines!

Oh, that charge! 'twas brilliant, splendid, and the con-
    test quickly ended,

And shook the tree of treason from its roots unto its
    crown

With a hurricane's wild power, sweeping, in a sudden
    shower,

Hosts of withered, blighted "'butternuts'" in utter
    ruin down!

Now the furious struggle finished, and excitement's
    heat diminished,

How the tired heroes slumber on the wet and muddy
    ground!

10

All but those, whose torches glaring through the
    woods are kindly caring
For our dead and wounded brothers, lying thickly
    strewn around.
Oh, my mother, *after* battle, when the volleys cease
    to rattle,
And no more is heard the shouting, or the stirring
    roll of drums,
When the mind is, for a season, gently swayed again
    by reason,
In the void, oppressive midnight, when reflection's
    hour comes,
How my heart aches for the dying, and the badly
    wounded, lying
Stark and helpless groaning, moaning in their pain,
    upon the ground.
And I think how each one's mother, father, sister,
    or a brother,
Or perhaps a still more *dear one,* would be smitten
    by the sound!
Oh, this killing one another is most wretched business,
    mother!
It is fearful to behold us fiercely shoot each other
    down;
And I'm sure the angels o'er us — blessed friends
    who've gone before us —
And the merciful All-father, must regard it with a
    frown.

Yet, as often as reflection turns upon the South's
    defection,

On her long and secret plotting to destroy the na-
    tion's life,

On her fierce, high-handed measures, seizing forts,
    and ships and treasures,

On her foolish, mad ambition to inaugurate the strife;

Then, I own, against the traitors — those red-handed
    violators

Of the peace of all our firesides — the authors of
    this war —

Who, without a provocation, stabbed a mild and lovely
    nation

With most murderous intentions, never knowing what
    'twas for,

That my heart, all hot and flushing, with combative
    torrents rushing,

Rises fiercely, without thinking of war's woes and
    wild alarms;

And then, to put them under, I would hurl all heaven's
    thunder,

Or gulf them with an earthquake, or call the world
    to arms!

Champions of a cursed dogma! chivalrous, if love
    of grog may

With the world pass current for that questionable
    grace;

Tramplers on a brother human! base defilers of black
women!

How I scorn you, pompous braggarts, how detest your
empty race!

I must close my letter, mother; for, you know, there
is one other,

One dear one who would sorrow if I should fail
to write

To her, whose presence gleaming, illuminates my
dreaming,

As I slumber round the fire in the silent camp at
night!

God keep that dear one, mother; may you always
love each other,

As I shall ever love you both through eternity's long
day!

And that God will kindly bless you, that no trouble
may distress you,

And we may meet once more on earth, your son will
ever pray."

PART FIFTEENTH.

———◦•◦———

Round and full the moon ascended, o'er the hill
    tops mounting high,
Pouring floods of glory earthward through the deep,
    blue cloudless sky.
Not a breath of air was stirring, all the landscape
    glowed with heat,
While, with watchful sense of duty, HARRY THORN-
    TON paced his beat.
Air and tree and field were silent; nothing, save the
    muffled tramp
Of the sentries and relief guard broke the stillness
    of the camp.
HARRY was serenely happy; letters had arrived that
    day
From his parents and MANOMIN, long detained upon
    the way.

All were well — had got his letters — prayed for him
    by day and night —
Grandpa felt so proud of HARRY — read his letters
    with delight —
" Thoughts of eighteen'-twelve would kindle his old
    face, and knit his brow;
He was then a brave young soldier, just as is his
    HARRY now ! "
Then MANOMIN'S tender missive fell upon his heart
    like dew;
All simplicity and frankness, trustful, passionate and
    true.
How her being yearned to clasp him — yearned to
    mingle with his life,
Yearned to form that perfect oneness — truly mated
    " *Man-and-Wife !* "
Then what wonder he was happy, truly loved by
    such a maid,
In return most truly loving — naught suspected,
    naught afraid !
Or that his rapt spirit, flying with the speed of glanc-
    ing light,
Sought MANOMIN'S little chamber, as he paced his
    beat that night ?
All her warm and ardent kisses rose unto his lips
    again,
And his veins glowed with soft fire, and his heart
    ached with love's pain !

Then her love flowed through his being like the incense of pure wine —
"Halt! Who comes there?" "Relief!" "Advance,
relief. Give the countersign!"
'Twas the guard that every sentry joys to know is
drawing near;
Sweeter music than their tramping falls not on his
listening ear.
Toward his tent did HARRY hasten — pray what
meant the gathered throng?
Something strange must be transpiring! Listen, what
a wild, sweet song!
Full a hundred awe-struck soldiers in a circle, sat
around;
GAFFER, 'tranced, was in the centre, standing upright
on the ground.
HARRY learned, upon enquiring, that, since fall of
early eve,
Witchful things had been progressing, hard for senses
to believe —
Drums were beaten, trumpets sounded, cymbals jarred
upon the ear,
When all knew no drum or trumpet, neither cymbals
were there near.
Lights had blazed from GAFFER's body — voices, calling men by names,
Had been heard, and several soldiers saw, within a
wreath of flames

The calm features of a comrade that had fallen in
    the fight,
Heard him say, "How are you, fellows?" then he
    vanished in the night!
Hands had travelled round the circle, stroking each
    upon the head,
When a band of unseen voices broke into a song,
    they said.
"Fellow-soldiers" — hark, 'tis GAFFER, in his trance
    state speaking, now;
See! his eyes are closed, and softly a pale light
    plays round his brow!
"Fellow-soldiers, all the lessons taught by earth's
    profoundest sage,
All the wonderful experiences from childhood to old
    age,
All the store houses of learning prized by wise ones
    of the earth,
Are as nothing to the lessons of this death and
    second birth!
I will give you my experience and 'twill answer for
    you all: —
In the struggle at Winchester I was wounded by a
    ball;
Stunned and dizzy on the instant I sank helpless to
    the ground,
While the warm blood trickled swiftly from the deep
    and fatal wound.

In a moment more my senses were restored to me
    as clear
As I ever had possessed them, and I lay there with-
    out fear.
I knew that I was wounded, badly wounded, it might
    be,
But thoughts of dying from that wound did not occur
    to me.
The battlefield, with all its noise, swam gently out
    of view,
And scenes of home, and boyhood days, and deeds
    my childhood knew,
Came drifting sweetly through my mind while there,
    without a pain,
I lay, and thought of friends I'd see when I were
    well again!
Sweet flowed the current of my thoughts, and peace-
    ful as the deep,
When not a zephyr stirs abroad, I sank away to
    sleep!
Anon I wakened, and beheld sweet faces beaming
    round!
I stood erect!—no longer faint and bleeding on the
    ground!
"'Why, how is this?'" amazed I cried, "'Oh did it
    only seem
That I was wounded, or am I *now* cheated by a
    dream?'"

Then looking downward to my feet I saw my body
lie

With white, stark face and rigid limbs, and glazed
and glaring eye!

Ah, then the truth that I had passed away from things
of earth —

Had crossed the dismal vale of Death, and found the
second birth —

Came pouring like a flood of light through all my
soul and sense,

And friends, long gone, now thronged around and
ended all suspense!

'Twas hard, indeed, to realize the fact that I had
died —

There bent the sky, there waved the trees, along
the river side,

Here were my hands, my feet, my limbs, my body,
and my head,

All clothed, erect and full of life! oh, no, I was
not dead!

Still, I had passed the dread ordeal, had drained the
fearful cup,

There lay my musket and I tried but could not take
it up!

I saw my friends, and thousands more bright ones
I did not know

Move freely through the ambient air where'er they
chose to go!

Now high among the fleecy clouds, now down amid
    the trees,
Now flying swift and straight through space, like ship
    before a breeze!
Oh, then a longing filled my soul to try a starward
    flight,
When instantly I rose in air, 'mid burnings of
    delight!
I drifted o'er the battlefield, where yet, in fearful
    strife,
Stood ranks of men with sole intent to take each
    other's life!
I watched the stricken, as they fell, and saw the pro-
    cess, grand: —
The body's death, the spirit's birth into this happy
    land!
The wild, bewildered, puzzled look as each his form
    surveyed,
Or turned his glance on field and grove, or where his
    body laid,
The gathering friends, the fond embrace, the joy, re-
    placing fear —
These are the first experiences of all on coming
    here!
When in my body, gun in hand, so willing to take
    life,
I little thought that overhead, spectators of the strife,

Hung millions of celestial ones with sadness in each
    soul,
To see man on his fellow man such tides of hatred
    roll!
And as I, too, hung o'er the field — made wise by
    my new birth —
My being wept at what I was and what I did on
    earth!
Then came a wiser one, and said, "'Be all your grief
    dissolved;
From out this fiery storm of war shall Wisdom be
    evolved!
Behold the sun, now shining down o'er river, sea,
    and land;
How green the trees, how soft the air, the prospect,
    oh, how grand;
But, o'er yon ocean's vast expanse behold the mists
    arise,
Sucked upward by this shining sun to darken all the
    skies;
Behold the heated air ascend o'er many miles of
    space,
While yonder, from the frigid poles, to take its vacant
    place,
Comes, charged with cold and thunder-bolts, the north
    wind, sweeping strong,
And o'er these peaceful scenes will burst in fearful
    strength ere long!

But when the angry storm has passed and shines the
    sun again,
The tree feels stronger for the blast and greener
    glows the plain!
'Tis so with man — success in life, prosperity and
    peace —
To feel his power and wealth and fame day after
    day increase —
Begets a grasping selfishness within his hardening
    heart,
That leads him to desire to seize a weaker brother's
    part.
This done then arrogance is born of such unjust
    success
And year by year does he contrive more victims to
    oppress;
Until, at length, *Harmonious Law,* infracted, once
    too far,
Asserts its potency, and lo! the land is filled with
    war!
But when its crimson tide has ebbed, its furious
    strength is spent,
The moral mind will treasure well the lesson that
    was meant!
And learn to know, as little drops wear out the
    granite fast,
So, envy, selfishness, and pride will lead to war at
    last!'"

He ceased, and swiftly I was drawn along a gleaming
    line

To where reposed, in slumber deep, a love that yearned
    for mine !

Her fair young face reflected forth her soul's deep
    dream of joy,

Her spirit rose to my embrace — she clasped her
    soldier boy !

But all in vain ! her waking sense was powerless to
    impart

That story of her spirit's feast to her enhungered
    heart !

For though to all we may draw near, as freely as
    we will,

That few are subject to control must be remembered
    still.

The how and why that this is so to me is not yet
    plain ;

A wiser one is waiting here, these riddles to ex-
    plain.

My soul is filled with joy and love to know, that
    out of strife,

I have emerged to glorious day, to sure, immortal
    life !

We have a fine, ethereal world, encircling earth
    around,

Where spreading fields, and flowery meads, and groves
    and lakes abound !

Where music breathes in every sound and fragrance
loads the air;
Where graceful trees profusely yield the flowing
robes we wear!
Let not these truths be shut away by doubt's obscur-
ing wings,
You only have the grosser forms, we have the soul of
things!
Behold the lillies of the field! no prince, in all his
pride,
Was e'er arrayed in robes so rich, so delicately
dyed!
Whence come your silks? from little worms! Your
linens? from a weed!
Your woolens? from a creature's back! Oh, wonderful indeed!
Whence come the luscious fruits you eat, the water
that you drink?
The air you breathe, the birds, the flowers? Oh,
doubter, stop and think!
Can God, from whom *all* blessings flow, so good and
potent *here,*
Come short, in all his attributes and powers in *our*
sphere?
Oh, no, the wonders multiply as *upward* you ascend!
And extacies and forms of bliss seem truly without
end!

God gives with an unsparing hand and every soul,
  that will,
At all the fountains of His love may freely take
  its fill!
Then fear not death, oh, fellow-men, no hell awaits
  you here
Except the hell you bring from earth, which soon
  will disappear
Beneath the genial floods of love that flow from ten-
  der eyes
On every erring child of earth that passes to the
  skies!
Your envy, pride and selfishness will then be buried
  deep
In earth with your lost robe of flesh, in everlasting
  sleep!
And all your higher principles will day by day ex-
  pand
Beneath the love of loving hearts in this celestial
  land!
Then fear not death, my fellow-men, but calmly wait
  the day
That shall announce your second birth. — Good night,
  I must away!"

PART SIXTEENTH.

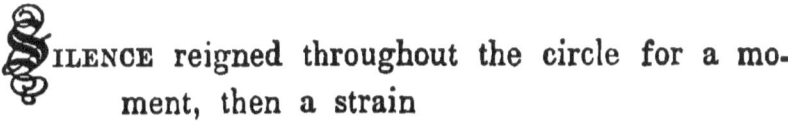

SILENCE reigned throughout the circle for a mo-
    ment, then a strain
Of the same delicious music poured its volume forth
    again.
Hark! what is that air, familiar, so distinctly floating
    down?
Ha, the circle add *their* voices! 'Tis the ballad of
    "JOHN BROWN!"
How the music harmonizes — falling soft each heart
    upon;
How the chorus stirs the spirit — "*John Brown's soul
    is marching on!*"
When the song at last was finished, lo! a presence
    bright was seen
By the side of GAFFER, looking calm and lovingly
    serene.

Robed in stuff of finest texture, band of gems around
    its head,

Oh, how thrilled those hundred pulses when in tender
    voice it said:

" Brothers, I have been enabled by your harmony
    to-night

To become *en rapport* with you, and be patent to
    your sight.

Rapport signifies *condition* — thus, if with your body's
    eye

You would view a given object it were waste of time
    to try

Until you are placed *en rapport* with it by the rays
    of light;

Light, then, is a fixed *condition* necessary to your
    sight.

What is light? 'Tis magnetism; 'tis the moulding
    law of God;

'Tis the life and love of atoms, Nature's great divin-
    ing rod.

As I said, 'tis magnetism — 'tis the law by which
    you see

Blocks and stones, or one another, fields and fences,
    flower or tree,

Yet intensest floods magnetic might pour ever from
    the skies,

And your spirits dwell in darkness, were you not
    endowed with eyes.

Yet the eye is not the seer, 'tis the spirit that be-
holds;

'Tis the eye receives the vision which the light reflects
and moulds;

And when you shall lose your body and your eyes
you still will find

That your light is magnetism, softened, deepened,
and refined.

Now each one of you behold me by this same magnetic light;

Let its silver cord be broken I should vanish from
your sight;

With your eyes you do not see me; close them and
you'll find it true,

Only by your spirit vision am I visible to you.

Through your ears you do not hear me, stop them,
and you still will find

Every sentence that I utter comprehended by your
mind.

That *effects* arise from *causes* is one of the sternest
laws,

And by GAFFER though you see me, GAFFER still is
not the cause!

He is simply a reflector by whose aid I turn the
light

On your inner sense of vision, this reveals me to
your sight.

And were not your minds receptive, did not harmony
    prevail,

From between us, I nor GAFFER could a moment lift
    the veil.

I perceive that you are asking in your minds the
    reason why

All men may not hold communion with the dwellers
    of the sky?

The solution of this question few earth minds can
    understand,

Though it is the simplest knowledge taught you in
    the summer land!

'Twould be hard to make a brother, born into exist-
    ence blind,

By description fix the colors of the rainbow on his
    mind;

Still I shall attempt to teach you why it is that we
    may come

Freely unto certain of you, while we cannot unto
    some.

First, remember, men are different, no two beings
    are alike,

And the truth of this assertion every mind at once
    will strike.

Walk some autumn through your orchard, raise your
    eyes, and you will see

A vast difference in the apples, growing on the self
    same tree,

Here is one all dwarfed and wrinkled, by its side
    one large and fair;
Both the children of one parent, nursed by the same
    sun and air.
So with men, from low surroundings some will rise,
    unfold, expand,
Crown their day and generation with a record great
    and grand,
While a child of the same parents in vile ways will
    take delight,
Die, and leave behind him mem'ries dark as Egypt's
    fabled night.
I refer you to the functions; though all eat, and
    sleep, and walk,
Have their bright and gloomy moments, laugh and
    cry, reflect and talk,
Do not all perform them different? Do you know
    of any two
Who are similar in these things, or like either one
    of you?
As by viewing Nature's functions we decide upon
    God's plan,
So the outward manner, surely, tells us of the in-
    ward man.
Note the child upon a journey ever meeting faces
    new,
It will pick the children-loving at a single inter-
    view.

Thus a self-hood of *conditions,* multifariously combined,

Is this wonderful immortal — crown of all created kind.

Not a single message, therefore, can the longing spirit send

Through a mortal whose *condition* is not suited to that end.

The musician that assayeth to produce a sweet refrain,

Every cord to proper tension is most careful first to strain;

Men are instruments of music — some with but one string are found,

Others two, and more another, tuned their proper notes to sound.

While we sometimes find, though rarely, those in whom each separate cord,

Nicely tuned, forever utters perfect sounds of sweet accord.

Now, as spirits cannot tune you, it is plain that they must choose

Those whose natural condition makes it possible to use.

Thus have I attempted plainly to impress upon your mind

The chief reason why we cannot use the mass of human kind.

But of vastly more importance to each brief sojourner
    here
Is the knowledge we would bring you from our
    sublimated sphere.
We have *truths* to give you, brothers, broader than
    your wisest give,
Truths that light the "'Dismal Valley,'" and instruct
    you how to live.
Man is not a fallen being; from the lowest forms
    of life
He has risen, out of tumult, out of discord and wild
    strife,
Out of thick and groping darkness, out of supersti-
    tions blind,
Out of bigotry, intolerance, and narrowness of mind,
Out of gross and cruel practices that long have
    stained the race,
Man has risen and is rising to a more exalted place.
"'By their fruits'" ye are "'to know them'" — and
    along man's path you'll find
Fruits abundantly attesting the progressiveness of
    mind.
Turn your gaze adown his pathway for two hundred
    thousand years,
Note the caves and holes he lived in, and his barb'-
    rous clubs and spears.
Huts and tents, and bows and arrows, rude canoes
    along the shore.

Are his only signs of progress for a thousand ages
more.

Then a glimpse of agriculture and of pastoral life
appears,

Which, with unperceived improvement, lasts a long
decade of years.

Then we find the clans uniting under *laws* for general
weal,

Notice also woven fabrics, gold and silver, iron and
steel,

Costly stuffs of silk and linen, famous for their gorgeous dyes;

Teeming cities, grander dwellings, and huge edifices
rise;

Swords, and instruments of torture, armors, shields,
and engines, dire,

That projected monstrous missiles and incendiary
fire;

Wars prevail, and cities crumble, new ones still arise,
more grand;

Ships loom up — man's mind is spreading o'er the sea
as well as land.

Slowly onward roll the ages, man expands from year
to year —

Hieroglyphics come and vanish, written languages
appear;

Startling truths, by bold proclaimers in the teeth of
error hurled,

Stir the rage of blinded bigots, and electrify the
world.
That earth, and all the shining stars, were planets,
huge and round,
And moved through space — though long denied, great
truths, at last were found.
The long, dark night that shrouded man at last came
to a close,
And 'mid the murmurs of the world the sun of
printing rose.
Then rapid were the strides of mind though fiercely
error clung
To her dark ways, and o'er all light her baleful
shadows flung;
She persecuted, cursed, and scorned, and raved in her
distress,
As year by year truth's sun arose, and her dark shade
grew less.
Now Freedom raised its head and bade oppression
lax its hand,
Then steam was born, and ribbed the earth with many
an iron band;
Then throbbing telegraphic threads bound shore with
distant shore,
Thus triumphed mind o'er time and space, on earth,
for evermore!
The planets all are sun-born things, and in the sea
of space

Swim round and round the mother orb, each in its
proper place.

Oh, many shut this truth away, and will not hear a
word,

Yet is it writ on every brood, and every mother
bird.

Eternal space is filled with God, and there was never
hour

When every atom did not throb with his life-giving
power.

He did not need a voice to call a *something* out of
naught,

Fruits of his life the gleaming suns were one by one
outwrought!

From every loaded orchard bough this truth is plain
to see,

Its shining worlds of fruit attest the God within the
tree!

Your sun, projected into space, unnumbered ages
rolled,

Convulsed and torn by laws that sought its functions
to unfold;

And when maturity was reached, its monstrous womb
was rent,

And forth into the realm of space a radiant child
was sent,

And ages, more than man can count, rolled onward,
morn by morn,

Until at length this earth of yours was, in its season,
    born.

And millions upon millions more of ages wandered
    by,

Ere Nature's forces ceased to strive, and dwelt in
    harmony.

In early days, ere cambrian rocks or cumbrian yet
    were formed,

With living, moving forms of life the shoreless ocean
    swarmed,

Thence slowly upward, age by age, progressed the
    mighty plan,

Until all types were grouped in one, and lo! that
    one was man!

Although his mind was dark and fierce, and knew not
    west from east,

Though *evil,* yet was he a *good,* considered with the
    beast;

The law that raised him up will still for age on
    age refine

The offspring of his loins until eternity shall shine

With love, and wisdom, and great truths, and things
    the good most prize,

Incarnate in a race whose source we vainly would
    despise.

And, brothers, when your souls have gained, within
    the body's case,

The sum of good that earth can give they'll seek a
  higher place.

And there will still unfold and rise, and rise and
  still unfold,

Expand with joys whose extacies no tongue has ever
  told.

The world doth make sad work with souls — insists
  that each shall take

A load of principles that lived but for the body's
  sake.

The spirit needs not selfishness, nor envy, hate, or
  fear,

Those are the forces made to drive and chain the
  body here.

And when the body falls to earth they surely will
  not rise

Along with love, and hope, and faith, and wisdom, to
  the skies.

But if your life on earth be bad — if good you do
  not seek,

Then will your spirit attributes indeed be very weak.

And what I mean by seeking good is strive to let
  your mind

Expand with sympathetic love toward your fellow
  kind.

Be not absorbed in gaining wealth — keep well this
  fact in view:

*All earthly honors, in themselves, are worthless trash
to you.*

Be kind and gentle in your homes; remember, love
is best

Developed in the youngling ere it leaves the parent
nest.

Decide opinions for yourself, yet reason deep and
long

On things profound ere you pronounce them either
right or wrong.

Think much upon your future life, and often of each
friend,

Who from your circle hath passed on to where your
footsteps tend.

Thus shall your life on earth be blessed, and scores
of tender eyes

Will pour a flood of love to light your pathway to
the skies.

I pray you, therefore, heed my voice; be patient in
the right,

Forgetting not your great reward; brothers, adieu,
good night."

—o○;●;○o—

PART SEVENTEENTH.

———◦◦———

Months wore on in Richard's dwelling—months
　　of mingled hope and fear—
All good tidings straightway darkened by the *bad*
　　they feared to hear.
War, they felt, was no respector—wise and noble,
　　good and true,
Quite as often as the vicious, fell before its bolts,
　　they knew.
Anxiously they watched for letters, and when "mail-
　　day" came and passed
Each would ask the inward question, "Will *this*
　　letter be his last?"
Oh, those letters were such treasures—read, re-read,
　　and read again,
Until every word and sentence became fixed upon
　　the brain.

All deserved a better record than this humble book
    of mine —
Sentiments most high and noble, glowing in each
    word and line.
Fine descriptions of the country which the troops
    were marching through,
Minute details of each skirmish, observations fresh
    and new,
Fillial words, so hope sustaining, full of tenderness
    and love
Toward each member of the household — trustful faith
    in God above;
Confidence in final triumph, though the sky so dark
    did seem,
Formed the burden of his letters — were his almost
    constant theme.
One June evening, while the shadows softly round
    the doorway crept,
And from off the blooming prairies smells of sweetest
    fragrance swept,
Underneath the spreading branches of a patriarchal
    tree
Sat MANOMIN, deeply thinking of the unborn yet
    to be.
RICHARD stealthily approached her, taking something
    from his cap,
And a moment leaning o'er her, gently dropped it
    in her lap.

How she started! how she clutched it! Then her
    eyes with tears grew dim,
Tears of joy too great to utter, joy to hear once
    more from *him*.
Then, with face suffused with blushes, swiftly she
    tripped up the stair,
And with palpitating pulses sank into the rocking
    chair.
Through her soul a storm of joy swept, making all
    her senses reel,
When 'twas o'er she lit her candle, and then broke
    her letter's seal:

" DARLING ONE, once more the pleasure of addressing
    you a line
That may keep you strong in courage and in love
    and hope, is mine.
Courage to sustain you, darling, should some rifle
    ring my knell;
Love to blunt the edge of sorrow, hope that all may
    yet be well.
Down Virginia's fertile valleys we are marching,
    day by day,
Over hills and through deep forests patiently we
    wend our way,
Through the dark ravines and gorges, over hamlet,
    farm and town,

Daily we go sweeping onward, like a freshet pouring
  down.

Into corn cribs, fields and orchards, houses, stores,
  as on we go,

Sadly does this living river every second overflow.

There are many things enacted which I do not
  care to tell,

War, at best, is wretched business, that I'm sure
  you know full well.

But there *is* a little story, interesting, strange and
  true,

That concerns our honest GAFFER which I will relate
  to you.

Yester evening, after sundown, in the fading twilight
  dim,

Having found that he was absent I went out in search
  of him.

We were camped near by a farm house, deeply set
  within a grove,

And, as if to further hide it, climbing vines luxuriant
  strove.

In the rear, enclosed by palings, with its tombstones
  glittering white,

Wrapt in peaceful, sacred silence a small graveyard
  met my sight.

Moved by some strong inward prompting I removed
  the wooden pin

That secured the little wicket, swung it back and
    entered in.

And although I closed it gently and walked on with
    muffled tread,

Yet distrustfully the breezes seemed to whisper over-
    head,

And the willows, bending downward, to the staring
    tombstones said:

"'Let us watch this Yankee soldier here among the
    Southron dead!'"

E'en the moon looked down suspicious from her win-
    dow in the skies,

Peering at me through the branches of the trees in
    mute surprise.

But I wandered on in silence down the shaded, grav-
    elled nave;

Suddenly I saw a figure stretched full length across
    a grave.

I was startled for a moment, then discovered by its
    clothes

That it was a Union soldier, still as if in death's
    repose.

Thoughts swept o'er me of assassins with foul pur-
    pose lurking near,

And I drew my "'Colt,'" determined I would sell
    existence dear.

But no murderous hand assailed me, triggers clicked
    not on the air,

So I carefully moved forward — heavens, 'twas GAF-
FER lying there!

Frightened, I sat down beside him, felt his pulse
and raised his head;

He was clammy, cold and rigid and I thought he
must be dead.

But he bore no mark of bruises, stabbed he certainly
was not,

For I ripped his vestments open and no mark of
thrust or shot

Was there anywhere about him, then the thought
occurred, perchance

This apparent death was really nothing but a spirit
trance.

So I sat me down determined that the issue I would
bide,

When a drowsiness came o'er me and I laid down
by his side.

Then my inner sight was opened and the graveyard
blazed with light,

While amid the foliage moving there were scores of
beings bright;

And I saw that standing near me, with his features
lit with love,

There was GAFFER in communion with a maiden
from above.

Oh, her radiant beauty, darling, was a glorious sight
to see,

And my spirit thrilled when GAFFER turned and
    brought her unto me.

Her tender eyes and loving look and faultless form
    and face,

Her silvery voice and winsome ways, her artlesness
    and grace,

The fascinating, thrilling touch of her angelic hand

Within my mind have crystalized that glimpse of
    Summer Land.

And never more can I forget the calm and holy
    bliss

Which renders life in that bright world so different
    from this.

Here selfishness, distrust and hate their promptings
    never cease,

There all is brotherhood and love, enjoyment, rest
    and peace.

My trance was brief and coming to and raising up
    my head,

Saw GAFFER in his normal state, who then in low
    tones said:

"Sit up, friend HARRY, close to me and hear while
    I impart

To you a tale that long has lain a secret in my
    heart.

A score of years ago my home was in this farm-
    house here;

I was a tutor from the north, employed by Hugh
    De Vere,
A rich, aristocratic man and proud as he was rich,
With many a thousand rood of land and many a
    bondman, which
He seemed to think endowed him with more virtues
    and what not,
Than could by any means belong to those in humble
    lot.
The very opposite of this his wife was, kind and
    mild,
With heart as tender and as pure as any little child.
She recognized the home of man and woman as on
    high,
And felt that all the aims of earth should be to learn
    to die.
She was a lady, nay was more, an angel of earth's
    sphere,
And like her was her only girl, sweet Adelain
    De Vere.
She and young Hugh my pupils were — she eighteen,
    he a score,
He but reviewed his Virgil and some things he'd
    learned before;
While drawing, botany and French and music she
    assayed,
And rising o'er all obstacles surprising progress
    made.

HUGH was his father's counterpart, full of that gassy
     pride
Which leads your pompous southern man to scoff at
     and deride
All honest men whose wealth results from toil of
     their own hands
And ever ruffianly parades his " " niggers " " and his
     lands.
I bore the arrogance and pride, the insults, taunts,
     and sneers
Of both the senior and the son for two long, bitter
     years.
Still not so bitter that I would not gladly take the
     pain —
Aye, twice the pain of those two years to live them
     o'er again.
For in those trying days there came a compensation
     dear :
It was the plighted love and troth of ADELAIN DE
     VERE.
And, HARRY, I had dived into my soul's inmost
     retreat,
Had plucked its choicest flower of love and laid
     it at her feet.
We met in secret oftentimes within this little wood,
Full well we knew the consequence if son or father
     should

Discover our attachment ere our plans were more
    matured,
That fearful insults by us both would have to be
    endured.
The time for which I had engaged was drawing to
    an end
And anxiously those fleeting hours I watched, you
    may depend;
For I had promised I would seek her father and
    demand
His sanction of his daughter's choice in giving me
    her hand.
And if withheld, as well we knew it was most sure
    to be,
Then boldly forth she had agreed to brave the world
    with me.
I'll not recall the bitter things that were that morning
    said,
Nor tell you of the vile abuse the son heaped on
    my head.
It is sufficient that I left the house that very day,
And that same night from 'neath this tree I bore my
    bride away.
Young HUGH collected a rough band and followed
    in our rear,
But we were made ""bone of one bone"" ere he
    could interfere.

In frenzied rage he bade his band burst in my chamber door —

A ruffian entered and got stretched at once upon the floor.

Then pistol shots flew thick and fast and wildly raged the strife,

My blood was boiling and I fought terrifically for life.

The bullets rained all round the room; at last, shot through and through,

I fell upon the floor, but not till Hugh was stretched there too.

Then came a blank and when at length my consciousness returned,

That Hugh was dead, my wife insane and I proscribed, I learned.

A score of men were organized to mete me out my doom

As soon as I had gathered strength enough to leave my room.

A colored maid of Adelain's had watched around my bed ;

To some asylum, far away, my wife was sent, she said,

And bade me, if I'd save my life, to rise that night and flee,

That in a wood near by she had concealed my horse for me.

By some strange luck my wounds had proved mere
punctures of the flesh

Which left me, when my fever passed comparatively
fresh.

This fact was gloated o'er by those who lay in wait
for me;

Already they had made the noose, and picked the
gallows tree.

I fled and shortly after heard my wife had ceased to
live,

Then sought I that seclusion deep which only woods
can give.

And there, 'mid simple hearted ones, rude children
of the wood,

I brooded o'er my loved and lost in deepest solitude;

'Twas then that spirits first began to swarm around
and give

Those tokens that when death ensues they do not
cease to live.

And often with my ADELAIN sweet converse I would
hold,

But not until to-night have I been able to behold

Her own dear self, and here beneath this huge old
trysting tree

She has in person met and pledged eternal troth
to me.

You saw her for a little space and many more
beside;

God speed the day that I may go and claim my
    angel bride.' "

Such is the story GAFFER told and such I give to
    you,

And only add I think it true and strange as it is
    true.

Now, darling one, I'll close this scrawl by bidding
    you take heart,

Be not cast down if years shall lapse and find us
    still apart.

The longest time doth close at last and round the
    hour will roll

That shall unite us evermore, one life, one love,
    one soul.

Be mindful of the chance of war, my life hangs on
    a thread,

A thrust, a shot, a bursting shell, and private THORN-
    TON's dead.

But still I have a clinging faith that yet down here
    below,

Stretch years of joy for you and me — God grant it
    may be so.

With prayers that you may keep your health, be
    cheerful, and not pine

O'er my long absence and great peril, I am forever
    thine."

PART EIGHTEENTH.

STILL surged the crimson wave of war, but the
whole country's face was turned
To Chickahominy's low swamps, where our brave
army's camp fires burned;
Where thousands of our gallant men sank down
beneath malaria's breath,
And like a fog before a wind were swept away to
sudden death!
For one long month in that low swamp did our de-
voted army lay,
While swifter than a battle's breath miasmas swept
our men away!
And by and by a furious flood broke o'er the treacherous river's banks
And rolled a turbid lake between our army's decim-
ated ranks.

187

On Casey's, Couch's, Heintzleman's small camps
    of isolated men
The sanguinary rebels poured the whole of their
    vast army then.
Oh, weird and wild the slaughter there, ten thousand
    of our brave men fell;
Why was this fearful battle fought, ah, who in this
    broad land can tell?
Why was a treacherous stream allowed so long to
    roll its waves between
That wasted army, when a child their awful peril
    might have seen?
Thank God, the rebels prospered not, fruitionless
    their bloody schemes
Were rendered by our gallant men. Brave Berry's
    glorious Wolverines
And York State's gallant hearts were there, and
    Keystone's boys, firm as her rocks,
And old New England's adamants that loved the
    fiercest battle shocks.
And there they stretched a wall of steel across that
    sanguinary plain,
Against which their wild sea of foes beat furiously
    two days in vain.
Hushed is the noise, decayed the dead, faded the
    flash of saber strokes,
But never will our land forget the fruitless slaughter
    of Fair Oaks!

For though in wild disordered mobs the rebel host
  was put to flight,
While thousands of their ragged dead outlined the
  boundaries of the fight,
And though all Richmond fled the town and all the
  South grew white with fear,
Yet "Young Napoleon" failed to march his army
  on their flying rear!
Though STONEWALL JACKSON, further north, by FRE-
  MONT'S heroes hard bestead,
Was paying all along his route a constant tribute
  of his dead,
And though the rebel JOHNSTON fell and LEE de-
  clared their cause was lost,
Yet paralized McCLELLAN lay with Chickahominy
  uncrossed !
For three weeks more he dallied on in that low
  country's poisonous heat,
And then occurred that *change of base* which seemed
  so much like a retreat!
The rebels heard with wild amaze this great strategic
  move of MACK'S
While hourly waiting in suspense his rushing column's
  fierce attacks.
Then bugles sounded, drums beat loud and ring of
  sabres stormed the ear,
And forth like bees from all their camps they streamed
  upon McCLELLAN'S rear.

Wild was the strife that soon began, for one long
    week by day and night,
Our wasted, weary but brave boys maintained that
    fierce, unequal fight.
The glorious deeds of those who fought in that ill
    starred campaign so well
I 'll leave for HARRY, who was there, in his long
    letter home to tell!

" DEAR MOTHER, once again I take my pen in hand
    to write to you,
To tell you I am safe, and of the dangers I 've been
    passing through.
For ere this reaches you there will the lightning's
    swifter feet have run
All through the land in haste to tell our bloody deeds
    of battle done.
And well I know that hearts at home will ache with
    anxiousness to see
This white-winged messenger of love come flying
    through the mail from me.
God knows I would not add one beat of Time's
    great pendulum unto
Your poignant seconds of suspense, so haste at once
    to write to you.
A long and fearful march we 've had, through wood
    and swamp, through field and flood,

One constant roar by day and night — a week's red
carnival of blood.
I cannot give the *full* details of those terrific days
of strife,
Those days of hunger and distress, those days so
prodigal of life.
I have not time to tell you now *all* of that long
and murderous fray
Nor *heart* to tell you of the scenes, the fearful scenes
upon the way.
Yet still I feel impelled to give such facts as came
beneath my ken,
In justice to the brave deeds done and hardships
suffered by our men.

Around Mechanicsville we lay with Richmond's gleaming spires in sight,
Hoping and praying every day for orders to begin
the fight.
There was a strength of conscious right in every
loyal heart that beat
In anxious hope before those walls, which would have
urged with rapid feet
The living bodies of our men, swifter than whirl-
winds' swift descent,
O'er abattis and rifle pits despite the storm of missiles sent,

O'er bastions, batteries and men, forward with resistless power

Until the " On to Richmond " bud *in* Richmond should
have bloomed a flower!

That longed for order never came but airy rumor,
with swift feet,

Went whispering round from tent to tent that we
were ordered to retreat.

One man amid that mighty host, one small, weak
man, aye only *one*,

Who 'd kept us in those poisonous swamps beneath
a scorching summer's sun

Till thousands of our best men died, now bade us
turn our backs and flee!

Flee from a foe we came to fight — flee from the
very task which we

Had left our homes and firesides, our wives and
children to perform;

In bitterness we turned away from trenches which
we came to storm!

We were not left to go in peace, for on our sullen
rear was poured

In long, deep, yelling, swarming lines the whole
exultant rebel horde!

We fought as only angry men, forced 'gainst their
will to shameful flight

By iron discipline of war — we fought as only such
can fight.

The Chickahominy still split our splendid army's lines
in twain,
The bloody tide from slaughtered men had flowed at
Seven Pines* in vain.
So when we came to Gaines' Mill where all our
army should have been,
We had to face LEE's whole command with thirty
thousand of our men.
Brave HEINTZLEMAN, and KEYES, and COUCH, and
FRANKLIN, HOOKER, KEARNEY, too,
The dashing, gallant, one-armed PHIL, so quick and
bold to dare and do,
Brave RICHARDSON's and SEDGWICK's boys, and SUM-
NER's lying far from harm,
Across the river, twelve miles off, in idleness at
BARKER's farm!
Oh, God! the agony of mind no human pen has
power to tell,
As sharp to those who did not fight as unto those
who fought or fell.
Oh, mother, fancy, if you can, our little army of
brave men
In long thin lines stretched o'er the field, from hill to
hill, and glen to glen.
From golden dawn to dusky eve lying beneath a
scalding sun,

---

* Fair Oaks.

13

Fighting a fierce exultant foe — outnumbered by them
   three to one,

When just within three hour's march lay sixty thousand
   of our boys

Chafing with rage at being held in hearing of that
   battle's noise!

In vain our brave men stood their ground and in grim
   silence fought and fell,

In vain our heated, well worked guns rained storms
   of grape, and shot and shell,

In vain our horsemen few, but brave, with naked
   sabres gleaming bright

Made furious charges on our foe, now on our left,
   now on our right,

In vain, in vain, while beaten back, our brave men's
   tears fell free as rain,

And rallying, still more desperate fought — oh match-
   less valor all in vain!

Our cannon one by one were lost until no longer
   one remained,

And while outnumbering us in front, the swarming
   foe our rear had gained.

Call after call for help was made, and as those dreadful hours went by

We strained our ears in hopes to catch the ringing
   cheers of succor nigh.

But all day long McClellan sat, far from all harm,
   with brow serene,

Unmindful of our fearful fate — great God above!
    what *could* he mean?

I will not blame him, mother dear, nor call him coward
    till I know

That he has been upon the field, and flinched before
    an equal foe.

Thus far *ten battles* we have fought and though he
    stigmatized McCall's

And Casey's men as cowards, *he ne'er heard the whiz
    of hostile balls!*

Though at Fair Oaks I saw that when our two days'
    bloody fight was done

He pompously rode o'er the field, past many a dead
    and wounded one!

But do not deem I wish to hint that he's a coward,
    e'en in jest,

I know not how he *might* behave with lines of bayonets
    at his breast!

But to my story, just at night loud cheers rang up
    the echoing glen,

And sweeping on with gleaming guns came French's
    and brave Meagher's men.

Ha! ha! how thrilled our weary hearts with wild
    delight's hot flushing flow;

And quick as thought our broken lines reformed and
    dashed upon the foe!

Ah, fiercely then the rebels fought, hushed was their
    loud, exultant mirth,

With but a dozen fresh brigades we might have swept
    them then from earth.

They did not come, but darkness did, and we aban-
    doned the attack,

Then came an order from our *chief* to cross the river
    and fall back!

Oh, then indeed our hearts were racked with most
    excruciating pain;

Obliged to march away and leave our sick and wound-
    ed with the slain!

All night we toiled along the road while thickly flew
    the rebel shell,

And every now and then some brave, true-hearted
    son of freedom fell.

Thus marched we on for six long nights, halting at
    every dawn of day

To plant our batteries and place our weary lines in
    war's array.

Then all day long 'twas roar and noise, and whiz of
    balls, and yells, and heat,

At night tramp, tramp! through swamp and flood, in
    silent, sullen, grim retreat.

At length one morn our heavy eyes were gladdened
    by a joyful sight:

The shining waters of the James reflecting back the
    morning's light,

Three hundred bristling cannon stretched across the
    slope of Malvern Hill,

And rows of rifle pits all dug which we were hasten-
ing on to fill.

Loud rang the cheers, for every man beheld this
vision with delight,

Assured that we had reached at last the termination
of our flight.

Right well we knew those silent guns the dirge of
thousands soon would sing,

And space for miles and miles around with their loud
bellowings would ring.

And proudly we could once more stand and say to our
exultant foe:

"'Come on and try the issue here, not one inch
farther will we go.'"

Oh, keenly does the private feel the stinging shame
of a retreat,

Keener than serpent's fang if he has not been first
in battle beat.

The shots may plunge, the shells may burst, and
bullets sing around his head,

The wounded fall and writhe and groan, the field
be covered with the dead,

Day after day the strife may rage 'mid winter's frosts
or summer's heat,

Yet bravely will he struggle on without once thinking of retreat.

And therefore when we reached the hill, we cried,
"'Hurrah, the die is cast!

Come on, you ragged rebel knaves, this chase, thank
God, has ceased at last!'"
And on they came in treble lines and furiously the
strife begun,
And you have doubtless heard ere this that it was a
most bloody one.
The rebels bravely charged the hill while from three
hundred cannon sped
All forms of missiles through their ranks and choked
their pathway up with dead!
Again and yet again they charged, and oft our gun-
ners would stand still
And for a moment cheer their pluck, then give them
grape shot with a will!
At every roar great gaps were made in their thick
ranks, yet on they came;
'Tis said that whisky, powder-drugged, their wretched
senses did inflame.
Straight on they marched in scorn of death, amid the
roar, with steady tread,
And cheered when they had got so close that all our
shots flew overhead!
Then from the rifle pits we rose, the cheering rebels
paused amazed,
And turned to flee — too late, too late, ten thousand
well aimed rifles blazed!
Oh, how they fell before us then, like autumn leaves
before a blast!

They could not form their ranks again, that charge
    had proved their best and last.
Now pond'rous shells came screaming up from gun-
    boats near the James' shore,
Which with our batteries and guns made old earth
    tremble with the roar.
In wild disorder, through the woods, the frightened
    beaten rebels fled,
And left behind them all their sick, their badly wounded
    and their dead.

The battle's smoke has cleared away, and left me
    without scratch or harm,
While GAFFER, brave and noble friend, received a
    bullet in the arm.
And PARTICK DEEGAN, too, I hear, was badly wounded
    in the thigh,
And though the wound is quite severe the surgeon
    says he will not die.
And further says, when he gets well *Lieutenant* DEE-
    GAN he will be,
For valor shown at Gaines' Mill, in charging on a
    battery.
But I must close this lengthy scrawl; best love to
    each and every one;
May God preserve you, mother dear, as He thus
    far has kept your son."

THE CLOSE OF THE CAMPAIGN—REST AT LAST—"LETTERS
FROM HOME!"—MANOMIN TO HARRY—HER PAINFUL
PRESENTIMENTS—"GOD KEEP THE BULLETS
FROM YOUR HEART, THE BAYONETS
FROM YOUR BREAST!"

———•◦•———

ALL hostile sounds were hushed at last, the fearful
    roar of arms was still,
No warm life blood in crimson streams now dyed
    the slopes of Malvern Hill.
The broken, beaten rebel hordes but late so fierce
    had fled dismayed,
No longer swarmed their threatening lines with flash-
    ing gun and trenchant blade.
The wounded all were gathered up and in those
    trenches lying low,
Gone to their long and last account, reposed the
    fallen of our foe.
Peace to their souls! for they were brave, mistaken
    true, but brave men still,
And to their madness freely gave all man *can* give
    at Malvern Hill.

Our own immortal slain were grouped in separate
    graves apart from those.
Yet narrow was the strip between a country's saviours
    and her foes!
To Turkey Bend our army marched and camped on
    James' grateful banks,
And sought the rest so long denied to its thinned,
    weary, way-worn ranks.
And though the plain that round them spread was
    low and sterile, black beneath
The scorching rays of July's sun, yet it did seem
    a goodly heath
To our poor tired heroes, who might eat and sleep
    and rest and dream,
Unsummoned by the long roll's call, or plunge into
    the James' stream,
And wash and bathe, aye frolic, too, untroubled by
    a hostile sound,
Ah yes, that scorched unlovely plain to them was
    fair and holy ground: *
"*Letters from home!*" rang through the camp. "And
    are there any, sir, for me?"
'Twas HARRY'S question. "Yes, my lad, you're
    lucky, sir, for here are three."
Withdrawn from prying eyes apart where nature his
    intenseness shared

---

* The leading facts and principal features of the description of the Peninsula Campaign have been taken from an article in "Harpers' Monthly," May and June Nos. 1865; by JOHN S. C. ABBOTT, entitled "*Heroic Deeds of Heroic Men.*"

His spirit reveled in the feast his far off loved ones
    had prepared.

His heart beat warm with glorious joy, obliviously
    the hours sped

As from MANOMIN unto him this letter o'er and o'er
    he read : —

"It is Sunday morning, HARRY, and the air is sweet
    without,

And through the trees before the door bright birds
    flash in and out;

Both your father and your mother and little JESSIE,
    too,

And one who loves you more than all, are writing
    unto you.

Do you ever think, dear HARRY, of the day when
    we first met?

Like a white robed angel that bright morn stands in
    my mem'ry yet!

Oh, I was but a wild thing then, decked out in
    beaded hood

And Indian skirt and moccasins, dark daughter of
    the wood,

Who loved naught but her fishing rod, her gun and
    light canoe

Until that ever blessed morn God sent her unto you.

But now my gun is red with rust, my fishing rod is
    broke

And all my Indian tastes and dress have vanished
into smoke;
For now I'm RICHARD THORNTON's child, the blessed
and the good,
And oh, 'tis meet I lay aside those relics of the
wood.
But still I love the wild woods yet and Ida's jewelled
shore,
And hourly wish the time would come when you and
I once more
Might stroll together as of old. Oh, HARRY, in my
heart
A light went out and left it dark when we were
forced apart;
And some prophetic inner sense seems whispering
in my ear,
"'Alas, poor child, that light shall ne'er be re-il-
lumined here!'"
Sometimes in dreams I see you stretched in death's
eternal sleep,
When with a cry of wild affright I waken up to
weep.
And then 'tis me that some fierce deed removes from
earth away —
Oh, why does this strange feeling haunt my breast
from day to day?
I *shall* be mindful of war's chance, and oh, I know
full well

That any moment but a "'thrust, a shot, or bursting
    shell'"

May rob me of the one bright form my soul so longs
    to see,

One warm, true heart whose priceless love is all in
    all to me!

But if a soul's most earnest prayers, put up by day
    and night,

Can shield you from disease of camps and perils of
    the fight

Then are you safe, my life, my love, for there does
    not arise

From all the murmuring lips of earth up to the
    bending skies,

Up through the thronging angel choirs, up to the
    Ear divine

A name so often born in prayer, oh darling one,
    as thine!

But notwithstanding all my faith fear's cold and
    anxious flood

Flows through the chambers of my soul like poison
    through the blood,

And sharp impressions of keen grief and trials I am
    loth

To think upon burn in my heart and fiercely menace
    both.

'Tis said the Sioux* are in a rage because they've
    not been paid;

---

* Pronounced *Soos*.

That they will rise and wage a war some settlers
    are afraid;
But they are so far south of us that we need have
    no fear,
I'm sure an army might be raised ere they could
    reach us here.
The farm is doing excellent, the corn is very fine,
The wheat and oats are heading out, the garden's
    care is mine;
Still I have leisure time to read and practice every
    day
And many of your favorite songs have learned to
    sing and play.
In freedom's service late enrolled are several neigh-
    bor's names:
GEORGE BANCROFT and young PERCY BARNES and
    gallant JOSEPH JAMES,
The brave young cockney HENRY COOK and JACOB
    PRETZLE, too,
Who burn to show Columbia what her foster sons
    can do,
Broad shouldered, stalwart JULIUS FROST, JIM DICKEN,
    trapper JIM;
No truer rifle pours its death than that which rings
    for him.
The two KINKEADS, the WHITEFIELD boys, JAMES
    SHOTWELL, true and good,
Son of that fine old man who lives down in the six
    mile wood

Hard by the shores of that sweet lake, where every
     passer by,
Upon the scenic banquet spread regales with eager
     eye.
All whom you love are well, HARRY, and send their
     love to you,
And pray your blessings may be great and hardships
     may be few.
You hope to get a furlough soon to visit us, you
     say,
Oh may God swiftly speed the time and hasten that
     white day!
To GAFFER give my kind regards, his story touched
     my heart,
Oh, I can realize the pain when ruthlessly apart,
Two souls that beat as one are torn by rude and
     ruffian hand,
And 'tis a blessed thing to know there is a better
     land
Where every wrong will be set right and all mistakes
     be known,
And every soul that seeks for love will recognize
     its own
True counterpart, true other half and they, a perfect
     ONE,
May live *forever* steeped in bliss, accountable to none!
To PATRICK DEEGAN give my love; may God's pro-
     tecting care,

By day and night, in camp and field be with him
   everywhere!
He is a noble gallant man, a generous hearted friend,
God grant unscathed he may be brought out safely
   to the end.
Alas, my paper is most full, oh, God, how can I
   close?
Would I could be transported too to where this letter
   goes!
Good bye, my darling, yet it wrings my soul to say
   good bye,
For now, *just now* I seem to feel an hour of anguish
   nigh!
Good bye once more; God grant I may soon hear
   again from you
Despite the whisper in my heart, " ' *This is your last
   adieu!* ' "
Oh *must* I close, my darling one? *May you be ever
   blest;*
*God keep the bullets from your heart, the bayonets
   from your breast!*"

PART TWENTIETH.

THE FRONTIER HOMES—FEARFUL RUMORS—ARRIVAL OF
HARRY—A TERRIFIC FIGHT IN THE DARK WOODS—AWFUL
MASSACRE OF THE THORNTON FAMILY—THE BODY OF
MANOMIN NOT FOUND—THE HEGIRA OF THE SETTLERS—
HEART RENDING SCENES OF MURDER—BATTLES OF BIRCH
COOLIE AND RED WOOD LAKE—CAPTAINS MARSH AND
STROUT—DEATH OF LITTLE CROW.

———•◇•———

THE waving grain was ripe and full and expectation's
heart beat high
At every Douglas County hearth o'er this especial
harvest nigh.
Those frontier farmers who had toiled so long, so
patient and severe,
Had lived in cabins rude and dark for many a weary,
weary year,
Subsisting only on such fare as could be snatched
from woods or streams
Now saw in their broad fields of grain the rich fruition
of their dreams!

The first rude cabin each had built, with rough, uneven
    puncheon floor,
With walls unseemly "chinked" and "daubed" and
    flat, trough roof besodded o'er,
Behind a grander edifice was now forever hid away,
Where, 'neath the gnawing teeth of Time it crumbled
    slowly to decay.
Their flocks and herds increased apace and broader
    grew their cultured land,
And from each passing year they wrung some meed
    of gain with horny hand.
Long and severely they had toiled but now they felt
    themselves repaid
For every extra hardship borne or every special effort
    made.
Indeed they deemed themselves quite rich, and care-
    less of the future's store,
Viewed most complacently the years now looming
    grandly up before !
Ah, false security ! how soon their hopes were mixed
    with anxious fears !
Then confirmation of the worst, then flight and terror,
    blood and tears !
For many days the airy tongue of trackless rumor
    had proclaimed
The temper of the sullen Sioux as daily growing
    more inflamed.

None but the nervous gave them heed and they soon
whistled down their fear,
" The Sioux! oh pshaw! too few! too far! no danger
of their coming here!"
And gaily they cut down their grain and gaily rose
their harvest glee,
As if such things as scalping knives and murdering
Indians could not be.
At length, as rumors grew apace, and some began to
heed the tale,
Came HARRY THORNTON from below upon the stage
coach with the mail.
Then for a moment the fierce tales of hatchet, knife
and fire brand,
Were quite forgotten as they rushed around the coach
to shake his hand,
" I'm glad to see you, friends," he said, "but there
is little time to spare,
The murdering Sioux have scattered out along the
frontier everywhere.
So I must hasten home at once; I thought to meet
my father here;
Alas, alas, I know not why, but I am racked with
strangest fear.
Will any one go with me home?" Three men stepped out, three true and good,
Stepped out at once with gun in hand and promptly
answered that they would.

'Twas Uncle DARLING and ED. WRIGHT and ANDREW
AUSTIN, all brave men

As ever made a rifle ring o'er lake or forest, hill
or glen.

The four set out, it was five miles, and through a
forest deep and dark,

And they had travelled half the way to THORNTON'S
dwelling house, when hark!

The ring of rifles faintly came borne to them on
the rayless air,

"In God's name, boys, let's hurry on, I fear those
shots mean mischief there!"

'Twas HARRY spoke and then each one went springing
on with speedier tread,

And presently they saw the house — "Hold on a
moment!" DARLING said;

"Quick! quick! there's Injuns! fly to trees! be cool
and cautious and take care!"

Just then six livid sheets of flame flashed out upon
the darkness there,

And six clear, ringing, loud reports awakened all the
echoes round,

And AUSTIN and poor EDWIN WRIGHT fell stricken
lifeless to the ground!

Swift as two tigers from their lairs sprang DARLING
and young HARRY out,

Six stalwart Indians drew their knives and rushed
upon them with a shout!

The foremost two went down at once before their
    rifles' deadly breath,
And HARRY quickly sent a third with his revolver
    down to death.
Another's brains were scattered wide by "Biting
    Betty's" crashing breech,
Then hand to hand they waged the fight, one Indian
    but remained for each.
The strife was brief, for DARLING wrenched the knife
    from out his foeman's grasp
And struck him dead, and quickly then his tomahawk
    he did unclasp
And rushing up dashed out the brains of HARRY's
    foe in time to save
The swift, keen scalping knife's descent that would
    have sent him to his grave!
They stopped not there for words or tears or com-
    ments on that furious fight,
But rushing on to THORNTON's house — oh, God!
    how dreadful was the sight!
Poor THORNTON, mangled, cut and slashed, lay stripped
    and swimming in his gore,
And ESTHER, stabbed and scalped and shot, lay dead
    and naked on the floor!
And ESTHER's father! oh, my God! how must these
    horrid deeds appal!
His head was severed from its trunk and grimly
    nailed against the wall!

Sweet little JESSIE, angel child, sure *demons* would
    have spared *her* life,
But these vile murderers cut her throat and stabbed
    her with a scalping knife!
MANOMIN'S body was not found, but smeared with
    blood her rifle lay
Across the threshold and they said, "She has been
    killed and dragged away."
Those were the six that now lay dead a few rods
    back there in the wood,
But oh, great God! it was too late, it seemed their
    death had done no good!
Whose pen can paint, whose heart conceive the rush
    of grief, the wild despair
That bleakly swept poor HARRY'S soul as he beheld
    the slaughter there?
"Oh Jesus! bend thy shining head down from thy
    glittering throne to-night!
Let all high heaven's pitying hosts look down upon
    this fearful sight!
And give me strength of heart and limb and eagle
    steadiness of eye
To run these ruthless redskins down and hunt them
    till the last shall die!
*Oh, God! how black this world has grown in one short
    hour!* can it be,
That I am left an orphan boy with none on earth
    to cherish me?

Oh, no! my blessed country stands with outstretched
    arms to claim her boy!

Yes! yes! I'm thine, Columbia! henceforth you are
    my only joy!

You are my father! mother, too! you are MANOMIN,
    all my life!

You are my sister! and oh, God! I'm thine for war
    and bloody strife!"

Then came the hot tears gushing forth—he wept
    as only strong men can,

And Uncle DARLING with wet eyes said, "Come,
    my boy! come! be a man!"

And with a mighty effort then he crowded back
    upon his heart

That bitter, scalding flood of grief that had so rent
    his soul apart!

Then for MANOMIN long they searched, they called
    her name but failed to hear

The faintest answer or response from any human
    being near.

No single trace of her appeared, no track of foot
    or shred of dress

To guide them in their anxious search or ease one
    pang of their distress!

They did not dare to linger long, reluctantly they
    gave her up,

Thus to the very brim was filled with bitterness poor
    HARRY'S cup.

A team was geared and in the box the bodies tenderly
    were placed,
When quickly with sad, heavy hearts their fearful
    footsteps they retraced.
They picked up AUSTIN and young WRIGHT and
    hurried forward to the town
To find a swarm of fugitives from up the country
    pouring down,
With tales of prowling Indian bands, of houses wrap-
    ped in flame and smoke,
Of mothers murdered, children brained, of rifle shot
    and hatchet stroke!
Oh, all was panic and despair and faces paled and
    hearts grew white,
Both men and women for a time were wild and
    helpless with affright!
But rapidly they organized; there were a hundred
    stalwart men,
And as they gripped their trusty guns they lost all
    fear of Indians then.
In four rude coffins, quickly made, in one broad grave
    were HARRY's dead
That night interred in DARLING's yard, and stones
    heaped o'er their lonely bed.
With Uncle DARLING at their head the settlers all
    now started out,
Expecting every mile to hear the ring of rifles on
    their route.

And every night they saw all round the glare of
    flames across the plain,

And flying fugitives came in to tell their tales and
    swell the train.

But one bright morn, with thankful hearts, they saw
    St. Cloud's white houses shine,

And one wild ringing shout of joy went flying down
    that lengthy line!

Their wives and little ones were safe, need dread no
    more the hatchet's gleam,

The sudden shot, the scalping knife, the Indian's
    awful midnight scream!

And they would take their guns at once, and reso-
    lutely turning back,

Would follow up the murderers' trails like blood-
    hounds on a victim's track.

They went, and oh! what tongue can tell the dreadful
    sights that met their eyes?

Young children's heads cut off and turned all ghastly
    glaring to the skies!

Bodies cut up and trees festooned with all their
    horrid fragments, there,

Girls disembowelled and on limbs hung tied together
    by the hair.

Great stalwart men shot down and scalped, their heads
    oft skinned completely o'er,

While their young wives in agony were nailed stark
    naked to the floor!

Small children's eyes dug out while each dark socket
   held a musket ball,
And unborn babes ripped out and spiked alive and
   writhing to the wall!
Oh, you, who walled within warm homes may safely
   seek your couch at night,
You cannot feel the deathly fear, the wild and
   withering affright,
That swept along that broad frontier, like prairie
   fires rushing down,
And drove a thousand households there all breathless
   to the nearest town!
Their grain in stack or shocked in field, and household goods behind were left,
And soon by Indian's torch of them were the poor
   fugitives bereft.
Their cows and oxen too, were killed, shot down
   wherever they were found,
And wantonly were left to rot where'er they fell,
   upon the ground.

Day after day the Indians swarmed and dogged our
   little party's track,
And at Birch Coolie in the night at last they ventured
   to attack.
But they were met by storms of balls that stretched
   their warriors in the dew,

And though they were a thousand strong yet durst
not charge upon those few!

All the next day they prowled around that little hand-
ful of brave men,

While from behind each clump of grass their rifles
echoed through the glen.

And all next night they hugged the camp and kept
their guns at steady play,

Ashamed and maddened that so few could keep
their thousand braves at bay!

And once that night with wild war whoop the Indians
to their feet did bound

And rushed upon the rifle pits the whites had dug
in circle round.

But they were met with laughs of scorn and such
a murderous storm of lead

That in a moment all the field was thickly spotted
with their dead.

Next morn some reinforcements came, the Indians
fled and were pursued,

And all along their bloody trail their wounded warriors
were strewed.

Two days they fled and on the third at Red Wood
Lake they made a stand,

For Little Crow* had joined them there with all
the warriors of his band.

---

*The chief of the Sioux.

Three thousand stalwart Indian braves against five
hundred of our men,*
But yet so burned their hearts with rage they took
no thought of numbers then.
At early morn, ere yet the sky was streaked with
red, the fight begun,
And oh! it proved to those vain Sioux a most disast-
rous, bloody one.
Fierce as a tiger HARRY fought, and though the
bullets whistled shrill,
'Twas mere child's play to one who 'd faced the rain
of death at Malvern Hill.
With glaring eyes he 'd watch to see some skulking
Indian show his head,
Then lightning like his "Spencer" roared and straight
the vengeful bullet sped!
Oft he and DARLING, side by side, would rush upon
some red skinned crowd,
And "Biting Betty's" ringing roar would rise above
the conflict loud.
Then crash of skulls and scattered brains, terrific yells
and hasty flight,
Would tell at once where those two men in fearful
earnest waged the fight.
For half a day the conflict raged, then LITTLE CROW
in 'error fled,

* Five companies of the Fifth Minnesota and about one hundred citizens.

But left behind him on the field vast numbers of
    his warriors dead.

Brave MARSHAL, straight upon their camps, rushed on
    his men that very night,

Four hundred prisoners he took and put the rest
    again to flight.

Of all the battles through the State I would I had
    the time to tell,

How STROUT and his heroic boys at Acton thrashed
    the murderers well,

Or give a record of the names of those who perished
    in the strife,

Like Captain MARSH, who was among the earliest
    ones to lose his life.

Or tell of Abercrombie's siege, where many an Indian
    bit the dust,

And thus to vengeance paid the price of all his mur-
    ders and his lust!

Suffice to say the Indians fled before the whites'
    avenging hands,

And o'er Dacotah's treeless plains were soon dispersed
    in little bands.

Where, ere a fortnight more had passed, old Biting
    Betty's sulphurous breath

Had stretched rebellious LITTLE CROW forever stiff
    and stark in death!

PART TWENTY-FIRST.

EVENTS FROM AUGUST 1862 TO NOVEMBER 1863—DEATH
OF GAFFER AT THE BATTLE OF CHANTILLY—HARRY AT
ANTIETAM—UNCLE DARLING'S LETTER TO HARRY—HE
BELIEVES MANOMIN TO BE DEAD—HARRY'S DESPAIR—
HE DETERMINES TO THROW AWAY HIS LIFE IN BATTLE—
HIS RECKLESS FIGHTING AT FREDERICKSBURG, CHAN-
CELLORVILLE AND GETTYSBURG—BATTLE OF LOOK OUT
MOUNTAIN—HARRY SHOT—HIS FAREWELL TO EARTH.

———◆———

UPON a huge old moss-grown rock that heaved its
    shoulders high and brown
On Minnetonka's* quiet shore two swarthy men were
    sitting down.
The eldest looking one had passed, by some few
    years, the prime of life,
But round, unwrinkled, only seemed to have been
    toughened by its strife.
The gathering "crows' feet" round his eyes, the
    drifts of silver through his hair,

---

*Minnetonka is the large and beautiful lake near St. Paul that forms the
headwaters of Minnehaha Falls.

Were nearly all the outward signs he gave of all
his years of wear.

His was a sunny, genial face, lit up by eyes of
gentle blue,

That beamed so kindly when at peace, but when
aroused would flash you through.

He was a tall, athletic man, broad-shouldered, powerful and straight,

And when he walked displayed great ease and natural
gracefulness of gait.

The other was a youthful man, with earnest, truthful,
large blue eyes,

Round limbed, well built, compact and strong, of somewhat more than medium size.

His rich brown hair curled closely round a finely
shaped, well balanced head,

And through the russet of his cheeks there glowed a
healthful tinge of red.

He wore the jaunty army cap, his clothes, too, were
the army blue,

He was as trim a soldier lad as e'er Columbia's
armies knew.

But through the sunshine of his face there crept a
shadow of distress,

Bespeaking some sharp inward grief which he seemed
striving to repress.

With heavy rifles both were armed and both looked
weary and way-worn ;

The garments of the elder one were somewhat tat-
tered, too, and torn —
" Well, HARRY," said the elder man, " 'tis time that
I was toddling back;
Your furlough's up, you've got to go, but I kin
foller on *their* track.
I reckon that atween us both, from fust to last, we
must have laid
A hundred of the cusses out. At that last fight
the way we made
The fur fly from their pesky hides I tell you now
want noways slow;
But come, my boy, give us yer hand, the sun is high
and I must go.
If no durned redskin gets my scalp I'll write ye
quick as I git back,
Fer may be I kin find some clue to put me on
MANOMIN'S track,
Fer, by old Goshen, I'll be durned ef I dont think
she's all right yit,
So don't look on the shaddery side, but brighten up
your heart a bit.
I reckon it'll all come right, ef't don't no use to
whine or sigh —
Take care yerself, old fellow, now, God bless you,
boy, good bye! good bye!"
They wrung each other's hands and spoke once more
affectionate good byes,

Then turned, and as they walked on, brushed the
    shining tear drops from their eyes.
Now southward HARRY's face was set, but oh, with
    what distress of mind,
His only joy the lingering hope that Uncle DARLING
    yet might find
MANOMIN somewhere, sound and well, and she might
    be preserved for him,
Though 'mid his sorrow's surging waves this little
    light of hope burned dim.
He weighed the chances o'er and o'er and sorrow-
    fully shook his head,
"Oh no, she could not have escaped, she surely,
    surely must be dead!"
Long time in silent thought he walked and just as
    St. Paul's spires gleamed
Full on his soul some inward joy some deep and
    quickening pleasure seemed
To light his face with radiant glow —"Ah yes, my
    GAFFER, why, oh why
Did I not think of thee before? thou link between
    the earth and sky!
Thou path by which celestial feet descend to loved
    ones here below,
God speed my journey to thy tent; the truth at last
    I then shall know!"
Poor HARRY! he had yet to learn that there was
    still for him in store

Another pang of poignant grief, a world of bitter
    trouble more!
For, in his absence many a field had by our " boys
    in blue " been won,
And many a grand, heroic deed at cost of precious
    lives been done.
GAFFER, his friend and tent-mate, he, who loved him
    as he loved his life,
At wild Chantilly's crimsoned field had fallen in the
    fearful strife.
He was a color bearer there and in the thickest of
    the fray
His flag defiantly was borne; he fell just as we won
    the day.
The losses on that hard fought field the country will
    remember well,
For there PHIL KEARNEY, dashing PHIL, and brave,
    impetuous STEVENS fell.
And many and many a soldier boy, dear to *some*
    heart in this broad land,
Came to his death in valorous strife to stay the sweep
    of treason's hand.
When HARRY reached the front at last, one clear,
    serene September day,
'Twas but to take his place at once in line of battle's
    dread array.
Yet dread no longer unto him; for death's menace
    he little cared,

Since there had not on all the earth one loving heart
to him been spared.
And so he begged for GAFFER's place and through
Antietam's* bloody fray
He bore the flag with flashing eyes till our brave
boys had won the day.
Wherever fiercest raged the fight, wherever fastest
fell the brave,
There, high above the flame and smoke was HARRY's
banner sure to wave,
But still amid that fearful rain of cannon shot and
shell and ball
Death mocked him, like a coy coquette, scarce vent-
uring near him through it all.
Three months sped on; our army lay along the Rap-
pahannock's banks,
Waiting to hurl its strength once more against fell
treason's bristling ranks.
Waiting to give, in freedom's cause, once more a
harvest of brave lives;
Lives dear to many darkened hearths, lives dear to
many anxious wives.
And there to HARRY came, one morn, the letter he
so long had prayed,
Yet now its privacy he felt scarce strength of purpose to invade.

---

*The battle of Chantilly was fought Sept. 1st and Antietam Sept. 5th 1862.

Oh, how the frost fell on his heart as this short
      sentence sharp he read:
"I've sarched the woods and from the signs conclude
      MANOMIN must be dead!"
His brain swam wildly and all earth seemed spinning
      giddily around;
Convulsively he clutched at space, then reeled and
      fell upon the ground.
He'd wandered off into a grove ere he had ventured
      to unseal
His letter, that no one should see what his emotions
      might reveal.
He did not faint, but nearly so; his heart grew cold
      and numb and still,
His nerves seemed palsied and divorced from their
      allegiance to his will.
But by and by his paleness fled, once more his cheeks
      their color knew,
And with his heart's pain in his eyes he read the
      dreadful letter through:

"We're back again, all safe and sound, cleaned out,
      but glad it is no wus,
I do not think the redskins come much nearer than
      your place to us.
They thar sheered off and went around and struck
      the prairie way below,

That Dutchman's claim at Maple Lake, and tuk the
    "'old trail'" road, I know;
And consequently nary house jest hereabout 'cept
    yourn was burned,
Though, blast their hides, they've done too much to
    make me love them, I'll be durned!
I went across to your old place to see if I could
    get some clue,
Some sign that daylight might reveal, of whar that
    gal of yourn went tu.
The house and stable both are burnt; oh 'tis too
    cussed bad I swear,
I tell you now, my dander riz at thoughts of what
    last happened there!
Now, HARRY, comes the painful part; the hope I had
    has now quite fled;
I've sarched the woods and from the signs conclude
    MANOMIN must be dead!
I found some bones picked clean and bare, some small
    leg bones, a hand and head,
And buried them down by the brook; oh yes, I'm
    sure the gal is dead."

Thus fell his last remaining hope and he determined
    in his mind,
If rebel balls would only strike, he would not long
    remain behind!

Next morning he was put to test: three times the
    engineers had tried
To make the string of pontoons fast across upon the
    other side.
But rebel rifles raining death, from Rappahannock's
    southern bank,
Had so appalled this corps of men that from the
    bloody task they shrank.
Then eight brave fellows volunteered and HARRY
    was among the eight;
Across the stream in open boat defiantly they paddled
    straight.
Now one, now two, now three went down, ere they
    had reached the sheltering shore,
But quickly finishing their work the eager men be-
    gan to pour
In living streams across the bridge, and mounting
    rapidly the hill
Instinctively deployed in line, and charged the earth-
    works with a will!
Then earnestly the fight began, far up and down
    that river's shore
Was one vast sea of rushing men, and cheer and
    flash, and smoke and roar!
And recklessly did HARRY fight; rushing where
    thickest fell the shot,
And though he envied all who fell and courted death,
    he found it not!

Then furiously he charged the guns and fought the
    gunners, hand to hand,
Yet still he fell not but was dragged away by one
    of his command.
For, all the valor of our men the bloody field had
    failed to gain;
"Fall back, fall back" the trumpets blew; five thou-
    sand lives were lost in vain!
Five thousand lives! and for each one some living
    heart would shriek in pain,
Yet HARRY lived who thought that none were left to
    mourn had he been slain.
Our army then re-crossed the stream, whipped by
    bad generalship alone,
For, by the *men* in no fight yet was more determined
    valor shown.
Then came a blank of five long months, five wretched
    months of fear and doubt,
When grave men shook their heads and said, "God
    only knows how 'twill come out!"
Then in the balmy month of May, in two commands,
    at dead of night,
Our army crossed that stream once more, a second
    time renewed the fight.
Two piteous days of fearful strife, two harvest days
    for reaper Death,
Who held high revelry amid that smoking battle's
    sulphurous breath;

Two days of seconds measured off by drops of blood,
from hearts that beat

The last life throbs of dying men, and then — what
then? *one more defeat!!*

Right gallantly each soldier fought, and HARRY, in
brave BIRNEY'S corps,

There on that field of Chancellorville outdid all deeds
he 'd done before!

When STONEWALL JACKSON'S furious men came sweeping down upon their flank

How lightning like his rifle flashed; and many a
headlong rebel sank

Forever down, to rise no more, before its withering,
upas breath,

His treason thus, in some small sense, made dimmer
by the sponge of death!

But HARRY lived to fight again; and soon at Gettysburg he lay

In line with BARNUM's * Empire boys, keeping the
rebel ranks at bay!

A July's sun hung overhead, blistering the very
earth beneath,

Tinging with red the battle's smoke that rose in many
a graceful wreath,

As if to twine about the brows of patriot spirits, as
they rose

---

* General HENRY A. BARNUM of Syracuse, N. Y., then Colonel of the
149th N. Y. Vols., raised in central New York.

At every battle throb from where their bodies lay
    in death's repose!

For three long days the air was thick with viewless
    messengers of death,

And heavy with the voided grime of half a thousand
    cannons' breath!

And every second men went down beneath that rain
    of shot and shell,

And all about where HARRY stood, his comrades every
    moment fell.

Yet not a hair of him was touched, for him no fatal
    missile sped,

He stood upon enchanted ground between the living
    and the dead!

With glorious victory was crowned this last, fierce
    effort of our boys,

And Independence Day* imbued with fresher cause
    for annual joys.

Not all the laurel wreaths that hung about the mem'-
    ries of that field,

Could unto HARRY'S mourning heart one throb of
    pleased emotion yield!

And now how burdensome was life, as idle days went
    shuffling by;

He only seemed to live but when in battle's front he
    sought to die!

---

* The battle of Gettysburg and the siege of Vicksburg came to a triumph-
ant conclusion on July 4th 1863.

But by and by an order came, and to the West he
    was transferred,
And heartily he prayed that now the boon he craved
    might be conferred!

November's morn was clear and chill and Lookout
    Mountain's base was blue
With old Potomac's veteran boys, led on by gallant
    HOOKER, true.
Three battle lines extended up the rough declivity
    to where
A long, high pallisade of rock frowned grimly down
    in silence there.
The Hundred Forty-Ninth New York, by gallant
    BARNUM swiftly led,
Around the shoulder of the hill dashed on with free
    and careless tread.
And from the rifle pits, like bees, they drove the
    rebels quickly out,
Then rushing up the rocky steep charged on the
    batteries with a shout!
They snatched five rebel ensigns down and captured
    prisoners in crowds,
While proudly o'er the rebel works their colors
    streamed, above the clouds!
And where was HARRY while that storm of shrieking
    shot and screaming shell,

Of rifle balls and sweeping grape, all round those
    veteran columns fell?

With blazing eyes and throbbing heart and firm set
    teeth and flowing hair

He bore, bare-headed, up the steep his country's
    dear old banner there!

He was the first to reach and plant his flag upon the
    mountain's crown,

And as he swung his cap and cheered a lingering
    rebel shot him down!

His comrades gathered quickly round and tenderly
    they raised his head —

" Oh sergeant, lift me to my feet, help me stand up,"
    he faintly said;

" Oh boys, this is a glorious morn! Away on Mission
    Ridge now shines

Our country's banner in the sun, and gleam our long
    victorious lines!

And here *we* are on Lookout's crown; below a mist
    the view enshrouds;

Oh, God! I thank thee for this death, in triumph
    here above the clouds!

Oh, sergeant, I shall soon be gone; I soon shall
    know a glorious birth;

Then raise me up a little more and let me bid fare-
    well to earth!

Dear mother earth, I loved thee once; thy roughest
    features once to me

Were lines of loveliness, but now I joy, old earth,
at leaving thee!
For many and many a month, dear earth, I've
walked thy bosom in despair!
But now, oh, God be praised, old earth, I'm going
where my loved ones are!
Oh, sergeant, see those shining forms, my sister,
mother, father too,
And thousands more I do not know; wait, wait,
I'm coming unto you!
Oh, comrades, let my grave be made above the clouds
up here in light!
Good bye, old earth — oh, boys, good bye — now lay
me down — oh, world, good night!"

PART TWENTY-SECOND.

THE SAVIOR AND THE SAVED—AN INDIAN LOVER—THE
CANOE JOURNEY OF TWO HUNDRED MILES—THE INDIAN
VILLAGE AT LEECH LAKE—MANOMIN'S WRETCHEDNESS
AND DESPAIR—MORE HEARTACHES THAN ONE.

———◦◦◦———

Now let us turn to that sad night—that night that
    HARRY clambered down
'Mid heart-felt welcomes from the coach, at Douglas
    County's county-town.
The day had been a sultry one and round and red
    the sun had set,
And RICHARD wiped his brow and said: "To-morrow
    will be hotter yet."
All day among his bending grain most resolutely he
    had swung
His heavy cradle, without rest, excepting when the
    whetstone rung
Its sonorous peans on his scythe, saying as plain as
    tongue could say:
"To work, to work, oh idlers all, be of some use in
    this your day!"

236

Across Lake Ida's surface lay the golden tresses of
the sun;
But shortening fast with every pulse, they vanished,
and the day was done.
With every outward door swung back no panel barred
the threshold, wide,
Of Richard's dwelling, or shut out the glimpse of
happy life inside.
The evening meal was long since o'er, and every
trace of it put by,
And all the household gathered round without one
cloud upon the sky,
The social sky, of their bright world, which goes to
prove, despite the din
Of brimstone clergy, heaven is found, and *only* to be
found, *within*.
There is not, neither can there be, in space's vast
dominion, wide,
An *outward* cause to curse the soul — its heaven or
hell must spring inside.
While innocently thus they sat, not dreaming aught
of harm was nigh,
Toward the house six painted Sioux were creeping
stealthily and sly.
Then sudden as the lightning's stroke there was a
blinding flash and roar,
And Richard Thornton headlong plunged, a bleeding corpse upon the floor!

With fury flashing from her eyes MANOMIN sprang
    and seized her gun:
Another roar and she, too, fell as murdered RICHARD
    had just done.
They then with hellish leisure, next, shot ESTHER
    and her father down,
And stabbed the child and cut her throat and snatched
    a trophy from her crown.
For whisky they then searched and searched, and
    finding none they stripped the dead
And gashed them horribly, and nailed against the
    wall the old man's head!
While they were rumaging the house, ransacking all
    the rooms o'erhead,
MANOMIN dragged herself away, for though shot
    through she was not dead.
Her absence they discovered soon and forth they fared
    to bring her back,
"Hush! hark!" and quick as cats they crouch and
    creep along the forest track.
'Twas HARRY's party drawing near, and stimulated
    by their hate
The Indians rushed to take more blood, but quickly
    met a murderer's fate.
PEWAUBEC, son of BIG DOG* had encamped that
    night on Ida's shore,

---

*Chief of the Leech Lake Band of Ojibways.

And as he walked toward the house was checked by
the first rifle roar,

And crouching down behind some brush he lay and
saw with inward pain,

The hellish deeds which he well knew he had no
power to restrain.

For had he been discovered there their frenzied joy
had passed belief;

Earth has no glory for a Sioux like scalping an
Ojibway chief!

When they went stealing off to meet the little party
in the wood

He rushed up to the house to see if he could yet
do any good.

The ghastly sight that met his eyes at once assured
him all was o'er,

When from the brush along the bluff that ran close
by the kitchen door

He heard a groan, and thinking first it might be some
Dacotah * snare,

He cautiously approached the spot; but 'twas MANO-
MIN lying there!

MANOMIN! how his throbbing heart sent the blood
spinning to his head —

He raised her as he would a child and toward the
lake with rapid tread

---

*Another name for the Sioux

He bore her tenderly, and laid her down upon a
    bed of furs

In his canoe, and speedily from its beach moorings
    loosened hers.

Together then, with moose-wood line, the two canoes
    he quickly tied,

And soon the savior and the saved were gliding o'er
    the waters wide!

When in the brush MANOMIN fell external conscious-
    ness had fled,

And now, as it came struggling back, she gazed upon
    the stars o'erhead,

And tried to summon the events of the past hour,
    but the pain

That darted through her, as she stirred, induced un-
    consciousness again.

There was a long point making out from Ida's
    timbered, eastern shore,

Due northward from the dwelling house and distant
    half a mile or more;

And when PEWAUBEO rounded this he turned his
    course toward the land,

And in a quiet little nook he drew the boats upon
    the strand.

Then with a woman's tenderness, softly and carefully
    did he

Lift up MANOMIN, couch and all, and place her under-
    neath a tree.

He plucked some "balm of Gilead*" leaves and
    bruising them expressed the juice

Which, in a curious birchen dish, he set one side
    for further use.

He then undid a roll of things† and drawing forth
    a linen sack

Tore off some bandages and put with care the precious
    remnant back.

A small bright fire next he built near by his patient
    on the ground,

Then with his hunting knife removed the garments
    from about the wound.

The second sternal bone was pierced and after tra-
    versing a line

Descending and a little curved, the bullet issued
    near the spine.

That it was a most dangerous hurt PEWAUBEC felt
    quite well assured,

---

*The balm of Gilead tree with its odorous, healing foliage grows pro-
fusely on the shores of Lake Ida, in Douglas County, Minn.

† The Minnesota Ojibway Indians — or Chippeways as they are sometimes
called — always make their excursions in summer time in light birch bark
canoes, and never set out from home without first making up a bundle of
things, among which will be found some clean empty linen bags to get meal,
flour, salt, or any such article, from the settlers when they reach the settle-
ments. PEWAUBEC — whose name signifies *iron* — was the only son of BIG
DOG, the chief of the Leech Lake Ojibways. Leech Lake was distant about
two hundred miles from THORNTON'S house on Lake Ida, due north, and the
numerous lakes between Ida and Leech Lake are all strung together by
connecting streams.   mm

And fruitful of sharp, shooting pains, and difficult
    of being cured.

He bathed it tenderly and dropped some clean bear's
    oil within the wound,

And pouring in some balm he wrapped his bandages
    quite tight around

Her bust entire, and then placed her gently in the
    boat once more,

Pushed off, and all that night he plied, without one
    resting spell, his oar.

When consciousness returned again MANOMIN lay
    some little time,

Perplexed to know if she was still on earth or in
    some happier clime.

Her ears were filled with songs of birds! how clear
    and soft and sweet the air!

While she was gently, gently swung within some
    fairy bower there.

All round her fragrant foliage hung, softening the
    percolating light;

Oh, had she then in truth passed through death's
    dismal, rayless vale of night?

If so, where were the radiant ones she fondly hoped
    would meet her there?

She listened, but no life but bird's was there apparent
    anywhere.

She turned her head: "Why, how is this? I'm lying
    in a boat, I see,

And on some stream, but moored beneath this low,
  thick overhanging tree.
Now I remember! oh, my God! my mem'ry serves
  me but too well!
So vividly that fearful scene, of where poor father
  THORNTON fell,
Cruelly murdered, who, good man, had never wronged
  a being yet,
Deep in the marrow of my brain is stamped, I never
  can forget!
But I was shot, what more was done, oh God, too
  surely I might know, .
All. murdered without doubt, but then how came I
  here in this canoe?
This is no vile Dacotah's boat! Oh heav'ns, how
  fiercely through my heart
Rushed all my wild Ojibway blood when forth those
  dogs of Sioux did start!
But I am rescued! and I know this is the *chemon**
  of a chief;
And my glad heart cries out "*megwitch!* †" to him
  who came to my relief.
For oh, I do not want to die until one loving arm,
  I know,
Shall clasp me round and one *dear* head bend o'er me
  lovingly and low!"

---

*Canoe.   †Thanks!

Her further meditations here were broken by a rifle
　　shot,
So near and clear it made her start, and for an
　　instant she forgot
That she was on Ojibway ground, moored in an ob-
　　scure, quiet stream,
And without meaning it she gave a half suppressed,
　　sharp, nervous scream.
There was a sound of bounding feet, a strong, swift
　　rushing through the wood,
The branches o'er her swung apart, and gazing through
　　PEWAUBEC stood!
She raised her hand but could not speak, but elo-
　　quently her dark eyes
Poured forth her soul's deep gratitude, not tricked
　　in affectation's guise,
But springing pure and unalloyed from out her being's
　　inmost seat,
Fell on PEWAUBEC'S thirsty soul like floods of heaven's
　　nectar, sweet.
"You must not move or speak," he said; "I've killed
　　a partridge and will soon
Prepare some broth that you may dine, for by the sun
　　'tis nearly noon."
He shut the branches and was gone and as his foot-
　　fall died away
She closed her eyes and thought how much she'd
　　reason to thank God that day.

PEWAUBEC had prepared his camp down near the
lake's white, wave-washed shore;
From where MANOMIN's boat was moored 'twas
distant twenty rods or more.
For here was water to be had and plenty of dry
driftwood, too,
Besides, an Indian always lies, if trav'ling in 't, near
his canoe.
With careful hand PEWAUBEC cleaned his partridge,
and the breast, quite fine
Chopped up with his sharp hunting knife, upon a
trencher of white pine.
All of the pieces of the bird into the kettle, scoured
bright,
He put, with water and with salt, then rubbed his
kindling wood alight,
And as the fragrant steam arose, a spoon he fashioned,
neat and small,
Of fine grained, delicate white ash for her to eat her
broth withal.
You should have seen him as he stood up to his
middle in the brook,
Feeding MANOMIN tenderly, a lover's fondness in
his look.
A lover's! ah, poor dusky child! chief, and a proud
one, though you be,
Although that maiden bears thy blood her *love* stoops
not to such as thee!

Between the one who holds her heart and thy grave
    nation's loftiest chief

A chasm yawns which all your love could never bridge,
    in her belief.

Two weeks and more with watchful care PEWAUBEO
    plied his busy oar,

Until the wigwams of his tribe loomed up, one morn
    on Leech Lake's shore.

With thick leaved boughs he'd canopied the boat
    wherein MANOMIN lay,

So closely woven as to turn the burning sunlight all
    away.

And over this, on rainy days long rolls of birchen
    bark he drew,

Also at night that her fair face might not be wetted
    with the dew.

Each night he bathed and dressed her wound with
    that fine delicacy and care

That marks the truly gentle heart, and is so winning
    and so rare!

He had forbidden her to speak so long as her pierced
    lung felt sore,

Therefore no word did they exchange in all that four-
    teen days and more.

His gun and fish spear yielded them a sure subsistence
    every day.

While luscious berries and wild plums were found
    abundant on the way.

And thus a fortnight flitted on, until, as I have said
    before,
The wigwams of his tribe loomed up one grateful
    morn on Leech Lake's shore.
While yet far out upon the lake sharp eyes his coming
    had descried,
And that an object strange he towed had quite as
    quickly been espied;
Out from that depth of giant pines the curious crowds
    came swarming down,
Along the gracefully curved beach and round the
    moorings of the town.
From little bays along the shore and every reedy
    nook and brake
Loaded canoes shot thickly forth to meet the young
    chief on the lake.
In hurried sentences he told the foremost ones what
    had occurred,
And bade them turn their boats about and tell those
    coming what they'd heard,
Then to the village hasten back and have an easy
    litter made,
Whereon in comfort might be borne the weary, wasted,
    wounded maid,
And have his wigwam cleared and cleaned, and with
    new mats the roof repaired,
Make ready some clean bandages and have some
    cordials prepared.

His orders strictly were obeyed and soon MANOMIN's
weary head
Pressed in deep rest and gratefulness the downy
pillows of her bed.
Right glad was she that her own sex her wants
henceforward would attend.
And speedily beneath their care her fearful wound
began to mend.
How fared it with PEWAUBEO now? Long, solitary
walks he 'd take,
Or all alone in his canoe would often row far down
the lake.
Within the garden of his heart, way down the long
ago, had sprung
Beneath MANOMIN's winsome ways, and the sweet
prattle of her tongue,
The hardy, climbing plant of love; and as it once
sought to entwine,
In after years, about *her* heart a frost pinched back
the venturous vine ;
A frost of dignified rebuke, a frost almost as keen
as scorn
Cut back the plant upon his heart, with many a
lacerating thorn.
For though this plant bears sweetest flowers while
'neath requited love it grows,
Yet beaten down, its thorns become sharper than those
which guard the rose.

And at that time she had not given to HARRY THORN-
TON the rich flower

Of her young love, which bloomed unseen within her
spirit's inmost bower.

But *now*, that their two lives were knit together like
a warp and woof

How could PEWAUBEO cherish hope? What could he
do but stand aloof?

But stand aloof and wait, and wait, with face so calm
she would not guess

Beneath his calmness writhed a heart in fearful
spasms of distress.

He so determined, and each day would take his stand
beside her bed,

Give her condolence o'er her grief and point to brighter
skies ahead.

Reminding her of coming joys, when war should
loose its crimson clutch

Upon the gallant soldier lad by whom she was beloved
so much;

And sing Ojibway songs to her, and daily thus per-
formed his part

So well, MANOMIN never dreamed that love for her
gnawed at his heart.

The ground was whitening o'er with snow, which
lodging on the evergreen

That garlanded those druid pines, made up a rare
and gorgeous scene.

MANOMIN daily gained in strength, and on this day
essayed to write

To HARRY, a concise account of all that happened
on that night —

That fearful night the murdering Sioux shot down
her dear ones in cold blood,

And how PEWAUBEC saved and bore her o'er two
hundred miles of flood.

She sent her letter to Crow Wing whence it was
posted on its way,

But never came to HARRY'S hand and never has,
unto this day.

The winter passed and with light feet came tripping
in the balmy hours,

With wreaths of sunbeams round their heads and
clothed in odors of sweet flowers.

Now every day, returning home, came Indians, singly
and in crews,

Who had been trapping down below, with fragmentary
bits of news.

MANOMIN learned the house was burned and all the
settlers had fled,

"Two men were shot down in the woods close by to
THORNTON'S house," they said,

"That very night," and then the thought, swifter than
lightning through her thrilled —

"We looked for HARRY at that time; it must have
been that he was killed!

"Oh, yes, it *surely* must have been, for now 'tis
seven months, and more,

Since I last wrote, and if alive he would have answered long before;

Who could the other one have been? Poor Uncle
DARLING, I've no doubt —

What would I not most gladly give to find this matter
truly out?"

About a fortnight after this the trader at that post
came back;

He'd been as far down as St. Cloud, and had some
papers in his pack.

He sunned away MANOMIN's fears, assured her DARL-
ING was all right,

That he and HARRY killed six Sioux near THORNTON's
house that awful night:

That DARLING had been over there and "ransacked
all around," he said,

And wrote to HARRY that he thought "from all the
signs, you must be dead."

"And when I told him differently you should have
seen the man's delight,

He clapped his hands and danced and laughed, and
wrote to HARRY that same night.

I saw the broad grave in his yard where all the
THORNTONS are interred.

ED. WRIGHT and AUSTIN are the ones about whose
  killing you have heard."
He told her of the different fights and "in them,"
  Uncle DARLING said,
"I reckon me and HARRY knocked a hundred red-
  skins on the head!"
"He is the only man but one who has yet ventured
  home again,
And when I left, ten days ago, he was just dragging
  in his grain.
Here are some papers I have brought, I think you'll
  find some news in them;
I see old GAFFER has been killed, that most mys-
  terious of men.
And Uncle DARLING bade me say, although as yet,
  no single word,
Since they had parted near St. Paul, from soldier
  HARRY he had heard,
Yet he was feeding on the hope of letters coming
  every day,
And the first one that he received he'd forward to
  you, right away.
But in the mean time while it seems as everything
  was upside down,
He thinks you'd find no safer place than in this
  little Indian town."
So thought MANOMIN and remained, and as those
  long, long weeks went by,

And brought no word from him she loved how oft
 she'd steal away and cry.

Often and often she had writ and why unanswered
 could not tell —

So powerless all her efforts were to break or pierce
 the mystic spell

That seemed surrounding her like brass; what was
 it? could it then be *fate?*

She would not grant it and resolved to curb her
 swelling soul and *wait!*

Wait with a quiet placid front while hope grew sick
 within her heart,

And nervous, gloomy fear usurped its chamber, and
 would not depart.

So sped the summer months away, and saucy autumn,
 bold and brown,

Scattering its coin of golden leaves laughed gaily
 through that Indian town.

The blackbirds sang their farewell notes, the lingering
 loons' adieus were heard,

And early snows on tiptoe came and yet from *him*
 no word! no word!

And in the stillness of the night, when she should
 long have been asleep,

She'd turn her face toward the wall and wring her
 hands and weep and weep!

And often through the day forget to play her calm,
 impassioned part,

And shadows, rising to her face, betrayed the dark-
    ness of her heart.

PEWAUBEO grieved for her but thought if there were
    deeper depths of woe

Than hope deferred, to wring the soul, that sharper
    pang was his to know.

Poor lonesome, wretched, heart-sick girl, how can my
    feeble pen, unskilled,

Portray her desolation when she learned her lover
    had been killed?

PART TWENTY-THIRD.

———◦◦◦———

"BRING here that stretcher! lively, boys! there's
    much to do," the surgeon said,
"This lad, though very badly hurt, has only swooned,
    he is not dead!"
They lifted up the wounded one and bore him tender-
    ly away,
And in a state of syncope for days and days poor
    HARRY lay.
The rueful, chilly weeks went by, now white with
    January's snow,
Now dripping with the rains of March, now radiant
    with the lovely glow

Of May's sweet presence, young and fair, then re-
    dolent and all atune
With glorious rose-breath, and the soft, sweet voices
    of the birds of June.
And day by day and week by week did HARRY'S sun
    of health arise,
And rosier grew his ashen cheek and warmer glowed
    his kindling eyes;
And soon at war's hot, flaming forge, with cheerful
    heart and willing hand,
Freedom's bold, skilful artisan, once more he nobly
    took his stand.
But now no knapsack weighed him down, he grasped
    his gleaming gun no more,
A captain HARRY had been made and pistols and a
    sword he wore.
Around "Lost Mountain's" rocky base, at close of
    one warm summer day,
Far down in Georgia, SHERMAN'S hosts ready for
    battle grimly lay.
The soft, round moon was climbing up the airy stair-
    case of the skies,
And quiet, dreamy stars looked down as peacefully
    as angels' eyes.
The surgeon sat in HARRY'S tent watching the moon-
    beams as they played
Among the rows of arms astack, when, turning sud-
    denly, he said: —

"I say, my boy, tell us the tale you've often promis-
    ed to, some day,
Of what befell you in the while that you at death's
    dark doorway lay;
Procrastination is a thief that filches time, is truly
    said,
So if you feel in trim to-night to spin the yarn,
    just heave ahead!"
"Most willingly I will, my friend, and 'tis a curious
    tale, forsooth,
Though valuable the more to you, who will be sure it
    is the truth:
After I bade adieu to earth a heavy, drowsy feeling
    stole
All through my being's avenues, and seemed to seize
    my very soul.
The mellow, rosy light grew dark, my dear ones'
    faces fled my sight,
And I seemed stranded, for a space, upon the death-
    lashed shores of night.
But gradually the light returned, again my dear ones
    gathered round,
And loving lips were pressed to mine and tender arms
    were softly wound
Around me in a close embrace, and fairy fingers
    smoothed my hair,
But *she*, whom I had *died to see* — heart of my heart!
    — *she was not there!*

As when, the heavy midnight air, a flash of lightning
    swiftly cleaves
And then the great, unmeasured void in deeper,
    thicker darkness leaves,
So, like a sword, this keen truth cut my spirit to its
    very core,
And left behind it a deep sting, far sharper than
    I'd felt before.
A deep, humiliating sense of how perversely I had
    tried
To rend this robe of flesh away without resort to
    suicide
Burned like a coal within my breast, and made me
    long for earth again
To bide my fuller time; but oh, I thought this hope
    was all in vain!
My guardians had perceived my thoughts, and that I
    stood there self accused,
Ashamed and saddened that God's love I had so
    foolishly abused
As to grow restive 'neath events Time's onward
    sweep had brought about,
And, like a wayward, fretful child, from life's great
    schoolroom had rushed out!
Then drawing near they gently said: "'Tis well
    your monitor reproves
Your headlong haste to wrench away your chains of
    flesh, and it behoves

You well to listen to its voice, and by the mem'ry
of your pain
Determine not strive against its plain admonishments
again.
Know, then, your body is *not dead*, and soon again
you will resume
Its dark habiliments, and all its obligations re-as-
sume.
She, whom you yearned for, is not here; it is not
ours to tell you more;
For doubts, uncertainties, mishaps are given to your
earthly shore
For you to battle with and solve, endure and yet
again endure;
They are the em'ry wheels of life that keep your
spirits bright and pure.' "
I now looked round me and observed I stood near
where my body fell;
I saw you feeling of its heart, and most distinctly
heard you tell
The stretcher bearers to make haste, and as they bore
it off, behold!
A long, fine line united us, brighter by far than
burnished gold.
"'Where'er you go,'" my guardians said, '"this line
will bind you to your form,
And, like the line that keeps the ship fast to the
anchor in the storm,

Will hold you firmly to the earth, where you must
    soon again return,
And for a further space submit the lower laws of
    life to learn.'"
My friends thronged round me, now, in crowds, and
    for a while, bewildered, I
Could only shake their hands and laugh, and laugh
    and shake their hands and cry!
I thought I knew what 'twas to feel deep, strong
    emotions sweep the heart,
But oh, a sense of that wild joy I know no words
    that could impart!
"'Come,'" said my guardians, "'time flies fast with
    you, who still are of the earth,
Come, glean awhile in fields of truth; come, gather
    gems of royal worth!'"
And as through space we sped like light with no
    apparent moving cause,
Much did I speculate upon this motion and its source
    and laws;
Which when perceived my guardians said, "'*We* move
    by the same law that you,
When chained to earth with clogs of flesh, tugged at
    by gravitation, do.
Whene'er you wish to move about your *will* says
    firmly, "'*go I must*,'"
And straightway it proceeds to *go* — dragging about
    its load of dust.

Hast never seen the acrobat, who springs in air and
    spins thrice round,
Alighting neatly and exact, square on his feet upon
    the ground?
If then *his will*, with all its load, shall move through
    space so free and swift,
Ought not *our wills* to do much more with no such
    weight of flesh to lift?"
We were now passing over groves, and gently-un-
    dulating hills,
Sweet little nooks, and tinkling brooks, and dancing
    waterfalls and rills.
Small lakes, as clear as mirrors turned their flashing
    faces toward the sky,
Fringed by tall trees whose trunks appeared like
    pillars of rich porphyry.
All of the larger streams were bridged by fairy
    structures of one span,
Whose fine material no words I know of could de-
    scribe to man.
Anon an edifice arose, far more than Babel towering
    high,
And stretching on through fields and groves further
    than scope of mortal eye.
Its timbers seemed like beams of light, finer than
    finest crystal glass;
Its architectural design the highest mind could not
    surpass,

Neither of earth nor of the skies, "for all the brightest
ones above

Contributed to raise this pile, under the inspiring call
of love, —

Love for the little still-born babes that come, like
spotless flakes of snow,

Each moment from some home of earth, whose darker
life they never know.

Here in this house — their "'Father's house of many
mansions'" in the skies,

These little throbs of Father God first learn the office
of their eyes —

First learn to *be*, to act and think, feel that they hold
immortal life;

But those emotions, strong and deep, perfected by
your earthly strife,

They lack, and never will possess; so envy not their
early birth

Into this life, but rather pray to grow and ripen on
the earth!"

Oh, God! it was a sight to see, from every quarter
of the sky,

The guardian angels flocking in to this great Found-
ling House on high!

Each in its bosom bearing up a little palpitating
gem,

But worth, in all its helplessness, more than the richest
diadem!

And this great play-ground of the spheres was all
    aflash with childish fun —

Here fair-haired Saxons leaped and played with Afric's
    scions of the sun,

And sweet Circassian girls and boys and dark-eyed,
    graceful youth of Ind

Mingled their greetings and their games, free and
    impartial as the wind!

It seemed to me I could have lived forever in that
    merry din,

Breathing the pureness of its life, drinking its holy
    spirit in.

But my two guardians bade me on, and soon we
    reached a radiant wood,

Where, vaster than the ends of earth, an airy, glit-
    tering temple stood.

"'Here meet the millions of the world that long ago
    have passed away,

The noble, wise and lovely minds — the history-beacons
    of their day!

Here are devised the thousand things that mark the
    progress of your earth, —

Here locomotives, telegraphs and telescopes sprang
    into birth;

Here all industrial implements, now used by man,
    were first bethought;

The secret of the camera was first within this temple
    caught;

And all the rising policies that mark the upward
    stride of man,

Up to the present hour of time, here had their rise,
    here first began!

Come in the lecture room and hear if there may not
    be some wise word,

Some priceless wisdom-gem let drop that will enrich
    you to have heard.'"

They led the way through leagues of aisles, arcades,
    rotundas, corridors,

With soft, warm, glowing roofs o'erhead, beneath,
    rich, noiseless amber floors!

Within the auditorium, vaster than earth's blue arch-
    ing sky,

Where seats, packed full of shining ones, ran round
    in ample circles high,

We took our place amid the hosts — both sexes —
    gathered there to hear

A treatise on Familiar Things, by teachers from the
    Seventh Sphere,

"'I see,'" one of my guardians said, "'your mind
    is not exactly clear

On how it happens *here* should be a lower and a
    higher sphere —

On earth the self same law prevails, and spheres are
    numerous there as here,

But oft o'erridden — wealth, sometimes, buying its
    owner a *false* sphere

*There are no riches here except the wealth of wisdom
and of love,*
*Each soul, unerring, knows its sphere when born into
this life above!'"*
He ceased, and then upon my mind the speaker's
thoughts fell clear and bright——
"'Thus have I tried to prove to you that naught
exists except the *Right;*
Eternal Father God *alone* fills all the endless realm
of space;
He is an integral of *Good*—for other Pow'r *there
is no place!*
*There is no special point in space where God is, more
than other where;*
Man braves the sea—while strangling him it tells
him plainly, *God is there!*
He leaps from off a precipice, and by sharp pains,
and broken bones,
Or loss of life, is told, *God's here!* in unmistakably
clear tones, —
Falls into fire, and is taught by the disorganizing
flame
That God is also present *there*, and is, as everywhere,
the same
*Great Living Order of All Things, against whom man
can never sin!*
Whose *Life is Law* — impartial, stern, and knows no
outward, no *within!*

Out from His life the planets sprung, as fruit from life
within the tree,

And *planet laws of life* have raised up man to immortality!

What soul was asked, *would it be born?* would it be
wakened into life,

To toil and sweat, 'mid doubt and fear to eat the bitter
bread of strife,

Blinded by Priestcraft, robbed by law, taxed by its
rulers for each breath,

Consuming tons and tons of life to be in turn con-
sumed by death!

And then, by the ""enlightened world""" when it
has reached this ""*far off shore*""" (!)

If not immersed, be damned by some, and *if* immersed
be damned by more!

Law, pitiless, impartial law, moved by the vital force
of God,

Developed Man from forms of life lower than ornament
the sod.

He comes, a puling, helpless babe, that may be barely
said to live,

And *how* or *why* he grows and thrives the faintest
reason cannot give.

He *grows just as the grasses grow*, no special law for
him was made;

He blooms, decays, he falls and dies, his *body* in the
earth is laid,

But *he* dies not, forevermore—he is the *ultimate* of life !

And will for age refine and rise, no matter through what line of strife

He has fulfilled the mandate, stern, that brought him on and off the earth,

No matter in what barb'rous age was cast the hour of his birth;

No matter to what creed he clung, or if he clung to none at all;

No matter whose poor slave he was, or who have trembled at *his* call;

He still is God's own darling child, the choicest product of His life,

And though he may for ages show the scars and bruises of earth's strife,

Yet at the last, refined and bright, his gladdened soul with joy will rise

And with hosannas unto God march up the causeway of the skies !

Go bear to all the ends of earth, wherever gropes a brother man,

And profer him these living truths, revealments of the mighty plan.

God raises up no *special* ones as *leaders* of the toiling mass,

All such are ministers of *Pride* — a worthless, self-commissioned class

Who, for the living that they get, load down the mind
    with error's chains ;

Cast off these *incubii — digest your mental food through
    your own brains !*

What is a dinner howe'er rich or life sustaining,
    worth to you,

To build your wasting form up, which some other
    stomach has passed through ?

On all beneath him man refines, and we in turn on
    man refine,

The highest working next below, clear up through all
    the endless line.

And naught is Wrong and all is Right———" here
    rang the trumpets' battle peal,

" Fall in ! fall in ! steady, my men ! *Fire !!* Now give
    them the cold steel ! "

A sad and bloody comment on the pleasant theory
    above —

A sharp, hard argument against the growing potency
    of love,

Was the fierce strife of headlong men that woke the
    echoes round that hill,

Whose endless, multiplying tongues like screaming
    devils screeched, *"kill ! kill !"*

*But still it is a truth for all, that will live on and shine
    for aye,*

*When deadly passions long have slept with all the low
    things that decay !*

———o○꞉○꞉oo———

PART TWENTY-FOURTH.

SHERMAN'S CAMPAIGN IN GEORGIA — FROM ATLANTA TO
CHATTANOOGA — SHERMAN'S GREAT MARCH TO THE SEA —
HARRY'S LETTER FROM SAVANNAH — THE END OF THE
WAR — HARRY'S LAST LETTER TO MANOMIN — HIS SENTI-
MENTS UPON THE ASSASSINATION OF LINCOLN.

———◦◇◦———

ONE hundred days of ceaseless toil, hard marching
  over hills and rocks,
Through forests, glades and swamps and streams,
  daily administering hard knocks
To treason's groggy, battered crown — more than two
  thousand trying hours,
And then our brave boys cried "Hurrah! Atlanta
  is forever ours!"
Upon Lost Mountain's rugged steep and rocky Ken-
  esaw's high crown,
At Smyrna, Camp-ground, Peach-tree Creek, was
  many a gallant life laid down.
But now the rough campaign was o'er, and a brief
  period of rest
Was granted to those faithful boys — our glorious
  Army of the West.

There, after wandering around, from point to point,
    and post to post,
For some two hundred days or more, like an unhappy,
    restless ghost,
Came Uncle DARLING's last brief note, informing
    HARRY of the place
Where lived that special presence he loved most of
    all the human race.
He dreamed not as he read with joy its rude, rough
    characters, that day,
The warm, true heart that coined them was a cold and
    lifeless lump of clay.*
His soul brimmed over with delight—he saw the
    unborn future's hours
Come tripping up, all wreathed in smiles and crowned
    with Hope's most precious flowers.
A constant, true and loving heart still hungered for
    him on the earth,
Still hoped and waited, yearned and prayed to be
    delivered from its dearth;
Still looked to see some angel hand reach down and
    save it from despair;—
The letter HARRY wrote that night was Heaven's
    answer to its prayer.
Oh, what a flood of earnest love, long pent within
    his swelling soul,

---

*See the article at the commencement of this volume headed "In
Memoriam."

Now poured its ardent volume forth along his letter's
lengthy scroll.

He told her all the fearful things that had befallen
since the night,

His reason trembled on its throne in terror at the
dreadful sight

Of mother, father, sister, all he thought that earth
for him held dear

Murdered and mangled horribly, ere he could reach
them though so near.

He told her how he thought *her* dead, and what a boil
his heart became,

And how he sought her at death's door through every
battle's smoke and flame!

"And when at last that door swung wide and with
swift feet I hurried through,

'Twas but to find a broader gulf was stretched between myself and you!"

He begged her to go down below ere winter should,
with icy hand,

Palsy the streams, or with huge drifts of blinding
snow blockade the land;

"For if you should not, oh, my own! no word of love,
the winter through,

No word to cheer our waiting hearts can be exchanged
between us two.

Then come below, down to St. Cloud, or better yet,
down to St. Paul,

And there in patient hope await whatever fortune
    may befall
Him whose uncertain pathway lies along war's dan-
    gerous, lurid track,
Who, having hold of Freedom's plow, until the end,
    will not look back.
Enclosed I send you names of friends, some comrades'
    families, who live
In good condition at St. Paul and who, I know, will
    gladly give
You room and welcome just as long as it may please
    you to remain,
So start at once, come down, come down; pray, let
    me not beseech in vain!"

Savannah's broad and silvan streets were swarming
    with our "boys in blue,"
Who said they'd come from Tennessee because they'd
    nothing else to do!
But on their path full many a heart, unhoused, in
    desolation wept —
A track through Georgia, miles in width, with war's
    red besom they had swept!
And HARRY, who with all the rest marched from
    Atlanta to the sea,
Was writing to MANOMIN there beneath a "Pride-
    of-India" tree: —

" My Darling — since I wrote you last, how have
the fleeting hours sped!
A hundred more historic days down Time's long cor-
ridor have fled!
Scarce had I mailed my last to you ere we were up
and in full chase
Of Hood's rag'muffins, who compelled our patient
army to retrace
Its footsteps many weary miles, that had been weary
once before,
And traces, all along the route, of many a gallant
action bore.
But not a single murmur rose from all those lines
of noble men;
Oh, if I *loved* our boys before, I *worshipped* the dear
fellows then,
Who with bright faces, willing hearts, elastic step
and cheerful shout
Shouldered their muskets, swung their caps and on
that backward march set out.
We followed swiftly, long and well our nimble and
now cautious foe,
But did not once get near enough to strike the vaga-
bonds a blow.
Around old Kenesaw's rough base we lay, when
gallant Corse's guns,
From Altoona's Pass poured forth hot iron logic from
their lungs.

18

Right gallantly we strove to reach the rebel rear ere
    they withdrew,

But getting wind of us, somehow, they raised the
    siege and off they flew.

Away to Kingston next we pushed, then onward, fur-
    ther, marched to Rome,

Then crossed the Ostenaula, still pursuing treason's
    flying gnome.

But our light, unencumbered foe kept well ahead of
    us, despite

The superhuman speed we made, and could not once
    be brought to fight.

Disgusted, we now paused awhile in Chattanooga's
    sumptuous vale;

And long, I fear me, will its rich, purse-proud in-
    habitants bewail

The day their fertile valley shook beneath our army's
    heavy tramp;

Scores of broad fields were quickly turned into one
    vast and noisy camp!

What foraging, for miles around! what gathering in
    of corn and meat!

Right well our army understood the value of good
    things to eat!

Nearly two weeks we rested there, recuperating beast
    and man,

Then breaking camp and shouldering arms SHERMAN'S
    historic march began.*

---

* SHERMAN'S great march actually commenced from the valley of the
Chattanooga, on the first of November, 1864. See his own official report
on this subject.

What shall I tell you of that march? There is but
little I can say,
As unimpeded we advanced a certain distance every
day.
The greatness of it does not rest on what we *did* or
how we fared,
But on the deeds we *would have done* — the unknown
dangers that we dared!
'Tis true we waded streams and swamps, built bridges
and laid corduroys,
But all such things, in times of *peace*, are common to
our western boys.
Our march was a great gala time, a pic-nic party,
the men said,
And well I warrant me that ne'er were pic-nic
party better fed!
Eggs, ham and bacon, poultry, lambs, butter and
honey, milk and cheese,
Rich golden syrups, apple jams, and all such delica-
cies as these,
Including ripe old mellow wines, peach brandy, bour-
bons and cigars,
Fit for a prince, nay better yet, fit for the proudest
of the czars,
Were found abundant in each mess o'er nearly all
that lengthy route,
For which we often had to thank our "'independent
bummer scout.'"

But often, as I lay encamped 'neath the great pines
    at close of day,
I thought with pity upon those whom we despoiled
    upon the way.
Many a cupboard we left bare, stripped many a smoke-
    house of its meat,
And many a little one, I fear, will beg in vain
    a crust to eat.
Such are the bitter fruits of war; oh, how I pray
    all wars may cease,
And folding up their crimson wings disturb no more
    the reign of peace!
I love the grandeur of the scenes each day before us
    have been spread,
The rich savannahs, graceful streams and tall pines
    chanting overhead,
Which have for centuries shook down their golden
    spindles and gray burs
Until it seems as if our feet profaned a soft, rich
    robe of furs!
'Tis sad the music of these woods, whose "deep
    diapasons" all feel,
Should jar with war's discordant sounds — the hoarse
    command and clang of steel —
That now, where ages, solemn hymns have only floated
    to the skies,
The bugle's slogan should ascend and smoke from
    hostile camps arise!

Your letter reached me, darling one, and its sad con-
    tents made me weep;

A little longer, and I hope the sunny hand of joy
    will sweep

Those cobwebs of our hearts away, and fill our beings
    with delight;

Hold fast your faith, my chastened one, day even now
    gleams through our night.

We're under marching orders, love; at every halt
    I'll write to you,

And mail the letters every time there is a chance to
    get them through.

Good bye, my own, and may the pow'rs of earth and
    air and heaven, above,

Protect you, shield you, keep you safe, my own, long
    suffering, patient love."

The war was over! yes, oh yes, the wasteful strife
    at last was done,

And Treason *crushed* and Freedom *saved!* and still
    the "many" were "in one!" *

Four years of devastating war — four years of battle
    and of blood —

Raids, murders, robberies by land and dreadful pira-
    cies by flood,

Four years of darkness and of doubt, distrust, anxiety
    and pain,

E Pluribus Unum.

And heart-strings tensioned till it seemed they'd burst
    asunder with the strain,
When suddenly, with crushing force, GRANT hurled
    his legions on the foe!
Sharp was the struggle, sharp and short, and sudden
    treason's overthrow.
Richmond was taken, LEE pursued, and soon he
    yielded up the sword;
JOHNSON surrendered—peace was gained—oh, peace!
    white-robed and blessed word!
Long may our children lisp thy name — palsied the
    tongue who'd change thee for
That seething synonym of blood, that word of dread-
    ful import — WAR.
At Raleigh SHERMAN'S army lay, with fresh gained
    laurels round its brow,
Its work was done — most nobly done — 'twas soon to
    be disbanded now.
And HARRY'S joy was deep and full, for oh, his
    coming bliss was near,
And by his own consent I give his last and joyful
    letter here: —

"DEAR MANOMIN — I am writing, calmly as I may,
    inditing,
On this lovely May-day morning, underneath a bloom-
    ing tree,

While beneath me flowers are springing and above
    me birds are singing,
And my heart with joy is brimming, my last letter
    unto thee!
Ere this note your hearthstone reaches you will know
    all that it teaches —
That " ' our cruel war is over ' " and rebellion crushed
    at last;
While upon Time's certain pinion, from sweet Cupid's
    soft dominion,
For us both, my little precious, days of joy are dawn-
    ing fast.
We are under marching orders — straight across Se-
    cessia's borders,
We set out to-morrow morning on our gleeful, home-
    ward way.
Now there is no foe to harm us, not a danger to
    alarm us,
And you'll feel me nearer, darling, with the ending
    of each day,
Until by and by, some morrow, that cold parasite of
    sorrow
That has wrapped your heart like net-work, shall un-
    fold, a blooming vine,
'Neath love's psychologic power it shall burst into
    full flower
As we kneel together, darling, and are rendered
    " ' thine-and-mine.' "

Oh, that day is swiftly looming, I can see it in the
glooming,

Down the future's murky vista, shooting up a courier
ray;

May its advent, then, be speedy, for our famished
hearts are needy —

Fainting for the rare refreshment to be served them
on that day!

All the blooming woods are ringing with the early
songsters, singing,

Though their music scarce attesteth half the ecstacy
they feel

As they revel 'mid the flowers in the warm sunshiny
hours;

So this letter to you, darling, will not more than half
reveal

All the length and depth of measure of the ocean of
my pleasure

Whose ecstatic, blissful billows in unceasing surges
roll

Through my being, grandly sweeping, then in softer
echoes leaping

With unnumbered, tender voices through the chambers
of my soul!

Still above my sunny gladness hangs a mournful pall
of sadness,

Heaping high with heavy shadows the glad temple
of my heart,

Through my spirit's essence stealing, seizing on the
throne of feeling,

While swift tears of vengeful sorrow from my eyes
unbidden start!

Noble LINCOLN! murdered brother! can the world
produce another

Whom, amid intestine passion every one would love so
well?

Who, though drinking hatred's chalice bore no living
being malice

And had often grasped in kindness the red hand by
which he fell!

Oh, how causeless, void of reason, was this last black
act of treason —

Striking down with devilish venom a true friend who
would have cared

For his enemies with kindness, with a tender mother's
blindness,

And much keen humiliation to the traitors would
have spared.

To the darkness of perdition will the annals of tra-
dition

Ever more consign thy memory, oh, fiendish J. WIL-
KES BOOTH!

Thou malicious, treacherous player, thou envenomed,
skulking slayer,

*Genius wipes thy name forever from her list of royal
youth!*

While a hymn to LINCOLN'S praises every coming
    minstrel raises
On all the earth's broad continents and islands of the
    sea,
And the angel choirs o'er us bear aloft the swelling
    chorus,
There shall nothing rise but hisses and anathemas
    for thee!
But, my darling, I'm digressing and my time, just
    now, is pressing,
So I'll turn again, though briefly, to the subject of
    our joy,
Every instant growing surer, out of sorrow rising
    purer —
For affliction is the touch-stone that exposes life's
    alloy.
I must close this little letter, and I grieve that 'tis
    no better;
Heaven bless you, oh my precious —— there! I hear
    the mustering drum!
Keep your lamp well filled and burning for the absent
    one returning,
Else before you are aware of it *the bridegroom will
    have come!*

PART TWENTY-FIFTH.

DESCRIPTION OF WINTER AT LEECH LAKE—A NEW CHAR-
ACTER—AN ACCOUNT OF MANOMIN'S FATHER—MANOMIN
MEETS A STRANGER—HEARS FROM HARRY—LOVE'S CROSS
PURPOSE—PEWAUBECK WITH A NEW LOVE—THE JOUR-
NEY TO ST. PAUL—THE RADICAL POWER OF LOVE—WHAT
MANOMIN DOES WITH HER MONEY—HARRY ARRIVES—
THE DOUBLE WEDDING—SONG OF THE MARRIAGE CHIME.

———◦◦———

WHITE, sheeted winter laid its glittering hand upon
    the murmuring lips of lakes and streams,
And silence reigned through all that icy land, save
    when the lynx-cat woke the night with screams,
Or fiery-eyeballed wolf howled through the wood, or
    Hyperbŏrēi struck their harps of pines;
And gracefully through that vast solitude, the trackless
    snowdrifts stretched their curving lines;
And not a bird, excepting now and then a moping ra-
    ven, toiling with cold wing,
To wake the frozen echoes of the glen or cheer the
    hope with promises of spring.

And bleak, and cold, and cheerless as that scene was
    poor MANOMIN's winter-driven heart —
No flower of Faith or tiniest leaflet green a hope of
    spring-time struggled to impart.
Three wintry months their ghostly robes had trailed
    past every wigwam in that Indian town,
For ninety days the shivering pines had wailed before
    the arctic tempests driving down,
Since that sad morning poor MANOMIN bent, with shiv-
    ered hopes, so low, her graceful head,
O'er the brief letter Uncle DARLING sent, that told her
    he, whom she adored, was dead.
Oh, God ! it was a moving sight to see the deep intense-
    ness of that young thing's grief,
So like a tender, young and blooming tree by stroke of
    lightning turned to yellow leaf !
But in those months, before the snows grew deep, from
    far Fort Garry* a young cousin came ;
A shy young girl, who early learned to weep for pa-
    rents lost ; MELLISSA was her name.
MANOMIN's father and MELLISSA's were the two sole
    children of an humble man,
Whose days were spent amid the spindle's whir, where
    streams of thread to eddying bobbins ran.
In great Manchester's busy hive was he an ever
    ready, uncomplaining hand,

---

* Fort Garry is the Hudson Bay Company's settlement on the Red River
of the North, known also by the name of "Selkirk Settlement."

A quiet, humble, steady, "busy bee"—a type of man
    peculiar to that land —
That land where few have *all*, the many *none*—all
    wealth, intelligence and lordly ease —
The few feed high on every luxury known — the many
    pinched for even bread and cheese.
Here GEORGE and THOMAS LEFINGWELL were born,
    but ere they had attained to man's estate
They held the fact'ry's drudgery in scorn and crossed
    the sea in quest of better fate.
Of bold, adventurous spirit, they struck out at once
    across the continent's broad face,
Where they would not be rudely pushed about by
    swarming, jostling seekers after place.
One married a Scotch girl, in Selkirk town, and first
    to trapping, then to trading turned,
The other one at Crow Wing settled down, married a
    bright-eyed Indian maid and learned
Firstly and foremost all the Indian ways, their tongue
    and superstitions and beliefs,
Their loves and hatreds, all their games and plays, their
    hopes and fears, traditions, joys and griefs.
And by shrewd sympathy in all their ways he bound
    them to him, with magnetic chain,
Which bit of strategy, in after days, contributed im-
    mensely to his gain.
This was MANOMIN'S father, and I've told how he gave
    up his life, one stormy day,

And left Manomin heiress to much gold, but what became of it I've yet to say.

The other was Mellissa's sire, and she, as did Manomin, lost her mother first,

And then her father, shortly after, he was slain one
morning by a gun that burst,—

A brash old musket which he tried to fire in celebra-
tion of the Queen's birth day—

But ah, that vitreous flint's impingement dire did "fix
his flint" and turned his joy to clay!

He, too, like Thomas, left his girl some wealth, an
education such as he had gained,

An honest heart, sound body and good health, a mind
in ways of truth and virtue trained.

Her eyes were blue as heaven's own azure sky, her
tresses soft and golden as the rays

Of autumn's sun, that tell when draweth nigh the mellow, dreamy, Indian-summer days.

And she, it was, who with Manomin, now, lived at the
mission house in Leech Lake town,

And strove to charm the shadows from her brow, and
sun away the white frosts, settling down,

Thicker and thicker daily round her heart, while
fainter burned the fire of her eye,

Until it seemed that some magician's art were needed
quickly that she might not die!

Time's pulse throbbed on, and northward came the sun,
and winter's legions struck their tents and fled;

Those days of painful silence were all done, and nature
   seemed arising from the dead.
But still the grave in poor MANOMIN's heart this glorious quickening did not seem to share;
Wherever else spring might new life impart there
   seemed to be no resurrection there!
But, like a spectre, sad and silent, she, the daily routine
   of her life went through;
Not one glad note or rippling sound of glee the un-
   strung spinnet of her spirit knew.
Far down into the depths of those dark pines alone she
   wandered, nearly every day,
And there, at one of nature's many shrines, for hours
   together she would weep and pray;
With sobs would say, "Oh, HARRY! do you hear?
   unbolt the door of your bright home, on high,
And let me feel your precious presence near, or rend
   away the veil 'twixt you and I!"
The spring time passed, the summer came and went,
   the buskined foot of autum pressed the ground,
And frightened streams, with purple leaves besprent,
   crept into every morass that they found!
On one raw day, when hung in sable hue of gathering
   tempests, was the threatening sky,
When courier winds their frosty bugles blew, proclaim-
   ing the great Arctic Monarch nigh,
MANOMIN, wandering, as her wont, alone, alike indifferent to dame Nature's moods—

Whether it froze, or thawed, or stormed, or shone —
    met, suddenly, a stranger in the woods.

He gazed at her; she cast her glances down, he paused,
    then turning back again, he said:

" I seek MANOMIN LEFINGWELL in town." "That is
    my name! what would you? I'm the maid."

Forth from his vesture then the stranger drew a letter,
    he had brought her from Crow Wing,

One glance! she seized it! "*God! can it be true!* " an-
    other look, and then the woods did ring

With a wild scream that made the stranger start, and
    poor MANOMIN swooned and fell to earth,

But with her letter clasped unto her heart, as though
    it held all life itself was worth!

There was a stream of water close at hand, and mak-
    ing use of his soft castor's crown,

The stranger bathed her brow till she could stand, then
    gently led her back again to town.

MELLISSA paled, and trembled with affright to see
    MANOMIN, tottering along,

Led by a stranger, and in piteous plight — her loosened
    hair swept down in tresses long —

Her waist unbound, while idly hung her zone — "*He
    lives !* " she cried and sank into a chair,

"*He lives on earth! Oh God! before thy throne I thank
    thee for this answer to my prayer!* "

With thanks from all the stranger went his way; he
    was a trader looking after fur,

And as MANOMIN's letter came the day he left Crow
Wing, he brought it on to her.

Now left alone she read, with heart aglow, that tender
missive through and through, and made

Decision instant to go down below, as HARRY earnestly
therein had prayed.

We'll leave her packing up her things and turn a backward glance — a brief one it must be —

Upon MELLISSA LEFINGWELL's sojourn at Leech Lake
mission, and quite likely, we

May find some matter worthy of our ken, some strange
affair of love's cross purpose, which,

The patient muse still smiling on my pen, may be arranged in this uncouth distich.

We dropped PEWAUBECK somewhere, on our track,
with a sad load of unrequited love,

But with a pride that kept confession back and lent
him strength to nobly rise above

The pow'r that binds so many others down, the pow'r
that makes so many fools, forsooth,

And gave this ancient adage its renown: — "the course
of true love never yet ran smooth!"

MELLISSA's eyes, as I have said, were blue, and her
fair skin was of a pinkish tint,

While her soft locks were of so rich a hue they would
have shamed the treasures of a mint!

And was it strange, when often left alone, PEWAUBECK
should have come to her relief,

Or they walk out and talk, in pitying tone, of poor
    Manomin's deep, destroying grief?

Or yet more strange, that in Pewaubeck's heart an
    azure orb of softness should arise,

That, in Mellissa's absence, did impart the same
    strange feeling as her own blue eyes?

Alas! alas! a tale too often told! Pewaubeck was a
    man, and man I find —

At least 'tis so maintained by sages old — *was simply
    born to love all woman kind!*

At all events he loved Mellissa well, and 'twas a
    thing most sensible to do,

And on no stony ground his passion fell — right heart-
    ily Mellissa loved him, too.

Now do not deem Pewaubeck fickle, nor that worse
    than no-sex thing, a male coquette,

Who, like a bee, sips sweets from every flow'r, till
    satiate grown, hums off in cold neglect.

For he had loved Manomin many years with all the
    depth and truth there is to love;

Yet not the pleading of his boyish tears nor riper
    eloquence her heart could move.

And lacking oil whereon its flame to feed, his lamp of
    love was shorn of its bright beams,

Which left his heart a charnel house indeed, strewn
    with the ashes of his early dreams.

How better, then, than yielding to despair, he, like
    the proud chief that he was, should give

His torpid love unto another's care whose warm affec-
tion bade it wake and live!
Nor deem MELLISSA played th' enticer's part — she
loved MANOMIN and with love was paid,
But in sad coin struck from a heavy heart, uncurrent
at Affection's Board of Trade!
It lacked the sonorous ring of the *true* coin the empty
coffers of her being prayed,
And that her trailing life-lines chanced to join those of
PEWAUBECK'S, who can blame the maid?
And thus it happened, thus it came about, as unex-
pected things so often do,
That where *one* wedding, even, was in doubt, there
seems fair promise suddenly of *two!*

MANOMIN and MELLISSA reached St. Paul upon the
St. Cloud coach, one chilly day,
And not a single incident, at all worth writing of'
befell them on the way.
As soon as they were quartered and got warm, had
bathed, and dined, and rested, and felt strong,
MANOMIN wrote to HARRY of the storm her shivering
soul had been out in so long;
It was a tender missive, I'll be bound, for you remem-
ber that it made him weep;
It was the one, you recollect, that found him at Savan-
nah, in his onward sweep.

Not much of note occurred to her that fall, nor yet,
    indeed, the whole long winter through.

One day poor Mrs. DARLING, at St. Paul, she chanced
    to meet, and for the first time, knew

That her heroic husband had been killed, and left
    behind her, in a distant State,

And at the news her soul with horror chilled, and grief
    her heart did deeply penetrate.

She freely gave the substance of her purse, prayed
    her to bear up under what fate willed,

And thank the eternal Pow'r it was no worse, that she
    and her two children were not killed.

The spring time came, and with it came a man, dark-
    eyed and swarthy, elegant and tall —

"Why bless my stars! it can't be! yes it can! it surely
    is PEWAUBECK, after all!

But oh! how changed!" his flowing hair cut close, en-
    robed in white man's clothes as black as soot,

His feet — well! well! would any one suppose an In-
    dian chief would ever sport a boot?

Oh, Love! you are a little tyrant sure, the strongest
    to thee bow the knee at times;

But since of barb'rous notions thou canst cure an Indian
    chief I'll bless thee in my rhymes!

It *was* PEWAUBECK, then, that came that day, and
    splendidly the noble fellow looked,

And from the "sea," her friends declared, straightway,
    no worthier "fish" MELLISSA could have hooked!

And glad, indeed they were to see him there, MANO-
MIN needed him to aid a plan
She had arranged with most elaborate care, but which
concerned a certain other man.
It was, to build upon the dear old spot, where she had
known so many days of bliss,
A handsome, snug and cosy little cot, and neatly fur-
nish it throughout, and this
She had more than sufficient means to do, her coin her
banker having long since sold,
And bought "5-20's," as she wrote him to, when
frightened coots $2.90 paid for gold.
MELLISSA, also, caused, at the same time, another cot-
tage, on her cousin's plan,
To be erected near, and 'twas no crime that she should
mean it for another man!
MANOMIN also had some tombstones and four rich
de-odorizing coffins made,
And then, with her own superintending hand, in nice
new graves, beneath a willow's shade,
She laid her dear ones near her cottage door, that she
might keep above them flowers in bloom,
And thus, while on the Earth-side of Time's shore,
grow more familiar with its gate, the tomb!
Events are crowding, I must crowd my theme — 'twas
only on this July that's just past,
When one bright morn MANOMIN gave a scream, and
cried, "Oh, HARRY! *God be praised at last* "

Ah, yes, indeed! the gallant lad stood there, — their
cups were full, their sorrows were all done!
There was a wedding shortly after where *two* pair of
souls were wed instead of *one!*
They took no wedding tour and needed none, but from
St. Paul straight to their homes they went,
Where, after all their generous wives had done, to
spend their lives there all should be content.
That HARRY was surprised and liked the cot his darl-
ing built and furnished, I've no doubt,
For does there live a sane man who would not? if so
please point this special wonder out.
And there they live, and there may they increase; my
story's done, I have no more to tell,
So, if you please, we'll leave them there in peace and
listen to what said their marriage bell:

SONG OF THE MARRIAGE CHIME.

" It is ended! it is ended! four existences are blended!
Never more to be distracted by uncertainties' dark
spell!
They are married! they are married! no love's promise has miscarried,
All is well, is well forever, all is well that endeth
well!
Time is fleeting! time is fleeting! Life, its lessons
are repeating —

What has happened will still happen, all the tongues
of nature tell,
God is living! God is living! and perpetually giving
Other lives to rise and marry, bloom and perish,"
said the bell.
" 'Tis no matter, 'tis no matter, whether, amid show
and clatter,
In a palace or a hovel your first throb of life began;
Flesh is mortal! flesh is mortal! just across the spirit's
portal
Swings the balance that shall weigh you, is the test
that tries the man!
There eternal, there eternal, 'mid existences supernal,
False or true, uncouth or lovely, every child of earth
must dwell,
Then I pray you, then I pray you, let no schemes of
earth betray you
Into shameful prostitution of your soulhood," sang
the bell.
"Love each other! love each other! every man on
earth's your brother!
Children of one common father, in the great stupend-
uous plan;
Then remember, then remember, you are an immortal
member
*Of the Fatherhood of Deus and the Brotherhood of
Man!*

I implore you, I implore you, ever keep these truths
 before you,
Search the chambers of your temple, every trifling
 vice expel;
Live more purely, live more purely, 'twill be better
 for you surely,
And eternal self-approval will reward you," said the
 bell.
"Truth is spreading! truth is spreading! and the
 ·beams that she is shedding
Fall in places long in darkness, reach the farthest,
 humblest hearth!
Creeds are falling! creeds are falling! Error's champions change their calling,
And enlisting in God's army help to renovate the
 earth!
There are millions, there are millions, there are billions upon billions
Of supernal bosoms thrilling with a joy that none may
 tell
That forever, that forever, with one God-like, grand
 endeavor
You have struck from dusky millions slavery's fet-
 ters," sang the bell.
"Time is sweeping, time is sweeping, onward, onward
 years are leaping;
Every soul that hears my chiming very soon, I know
 full well

In the boundless ether o'er us, with the many gone
    before us,
Will be marching to the music of eternity's great
    bell.
So adieu then, so adieu then, oh, I pray you to be
    true men!
Reaching upward, upward, upward,— ever striving to
    excel—
Rising higher, rising higher, when your lives on earth
    expire,
Marching grandly up the pathway of the ages," closed
    the bell.

THE END.

www.ingramcontent.com/pod-product-compliance
Lightning Source LLC
Chambersburg PA
CBHW060548030726
47498CB00005B/1307